With Malice Toward Some

Box 115, Superior, WI 54880 (715) 394-9513

With Malice Toward Some

Very Short Stories for Very Busy People

Georgia Post

First Edition

Copyright 2004, Georgia Post

Cover design: Saydi Kaufman

All rights reserved, including the right to reproduce this book or portions thereof, in any form, except for brief quotations embodied in articles and reviews, without written permission from the publisher. This is a work of fiction. Any resemblance to real persons is purely coincidental.

ISBN Number 1-886028-65-6

Library of Congress Catalog Card Number: 2004111151

Published by:

Savage Press
P.O. Box 115
Superior, WI 54880

Phone: 715-394-9513

E-mail: mail@savpress.com

Web Site: www.savpress.com

Printed in the USA

With affection and appreciation to:

The Tarpon Springs Writers Group, who critiqued with sincerity and then gently pushed and shoved.

Vass Gardiakos, who nagged me until I went to the Tarpon Springs Writers Group.

John Paris, who mentored long distance Spartan style.

Jill Rhodes, who tactfully edited and typed.

Trudy Knox, who insisted I could make this book happen and gave me 809 "how to" suggestions.

And especially to:
my husband, Zenon, who made it all possible.
He surrendered the computer.

One of these stories is true.

With Malice Toward Some

The Dead Horse in the Bathtub

I tried to get my husband's attention. He would come home every day and automatically ask me what was new. I would tell him, and he would reply. The conversation, such as it was, went like this:

"I shopped at the supermarket today."

"Really?"

"The dry cleaners delivered your jacket today."

"Great."

"I played bridge at the club."

"That's nice."

"I had my hair done."

"Terrific."

No, I am not employed. It would not do for the junior partner's wife to have a job. However, I do volunteer at the local hospital twice a week. Still, life was a day-to-day bore.

Then I heard this story about the dead horse in the bathtub. You know, the one where the wife wants to finally tell her husband what's new, so she pays someone to put a dead horse in the tub. I got to fantasizing about what could be new. It provided me with a much-needed daily purpose.

I began to scheme. I started off slowly. The next time my husband asked what was new I said, "I am thinking of robbing a bank."

"That's nice," he replied. "What's for dinner?"

See what I mean?

The next time he asked what was new I told him, "I bought a Saturday night special at a pawnshop."

"That's interesting. Do you want to go to a movie tonight?" he replied.

So I decided I really would rob a bank. I planned it carefully. No weapons. Preferably a small haul so that it would count as a misdemeanor, a first time offense. I bought a gorgeous blond wig at the local flea market along with a black leather jacket and black running shoes. A pair of jeans completed the disguise. I was ready.

I approached the bank with a note I had pieced together to give to the bank teller. It said: "Do not be alarmed. All I want is $97."

As the teller read the note, I said in a low voice, "My partner over there" (I pointed to a customer filling out a withdrawal form) "is high strung and is hiding a gun that is aimed at you. Don't be stupid over $97."

Guess what? She counted out $97.

I left quickly while "my partner" strolled into line for his transaction. Just enough time for me to run around the corner of the bank and be seen leaving as a gorgeous blond in black running shoes. I quickly removed the wig, jacket, and shoes and placed them in a bag that contained a pair of patent pumps. The bag was reversible. Yellow polka dots on a black background to carry in the bank, now plain black.

I then quickly walked around the corner again, back to the bank, looking like a customer. Of course, confusion was everywhere.

When my husband came home that evening and asked me what was new, I pointed to the TV. I was on the six o'clock news captured by the bank camera. A gorgeous blond in a black leather jacket and black running shoes.

My husband recognized me.

I have his full attention now. It will be a long time before he asks me what's new. When he does, I will be ready.

A Good Wife

The visitor hesitated before asking, "How are you feeling today, Mrs. Webb? I just saw your husband."

Mrs. Webb sighed and thought, "Why can't they leave me alone?"

"You have been married 23 years, right?"

A deep breath. "Yes. 23 years."

"I just got married myself, Mrs. Webb. I bet you have some secrets that kept you married so long."

"Well," replied Mrs. Webb, "if you want to know the truth, on my wedding day my mother gave me the secret to a happy marriage. She said that to keep your husband happy, you have to be whatever he wants, when he wants.

"It started as a game on our honeymoon. I asked him who he would like me to be that day. He said he wanted me to be his Lolita. So I tried. After all, it was my wedding day. The next day he wanted to play the game again. And he asked me to be his golf buddy.

"I said, 'Okay.'

"Then he got pushy. He would say, 'Be my accountant,' and together we would do the budget or go to the bank. I would say, 'Okay.'

"Or he would say, 'Be my best friend. Let's go bowling together.' 'Okay.' Sometimes he would ask me to be his chauffeur, and we would drive to the casino in Jersey. Some days I was his mistress, and we would go shopping at Victoria's Secret before we went to the Ramada Inn.

"Thursdays were tricky. It was my grocery shopping day. Sometimes he would ask me to be his cooking teacher. We would go to specialty markets and shop. Fridays were easy. It was my day to be a wife and pick the restaurant and movie.

"Saturdays were very hard. They were busy. Saturdays were his 'anything goes' days, and, believe me, when it was over, we were always really tired.

"Sundays were quiet. We would be so tired from Saturdays that we just relaxed. I tried to keep out of his way.

"This went on for a long time. Then, one Sunday I made a mistake. I didn't keep out of his way. He asked me who I was going to be that day. So I told him, 'I am going to be myself today.' He got really mad! Then I got mad. So I shot him.

"They called it attempted murder. I'll be out in about nine years."

With Malice Toward Some

The Acura Revenge

I had a tough time saving up enough money to buy the 1974 Acura Legend. It was my passion. When it was stolen the first time, the insurance company settled without a fight. The car was still worth $40,000, so the $18,000 claim was approved. The second time it was stolen it was almost totaled. The insurance check barely covered the repairs. I was really pissed.

The cops who recovered the car told me a car like that attracted attention no matter where it was parked. It was just one of those cars in demand. Get rid of it, they advised. I couldn't. I had worked too hard to get it.

There had to be a solution. Alarms and locking the steering wheel, things like that offered little protection. "Well," I thought, "if I can't protect the car, I can at least get the thief."

I got together with a friend of mine who worked in the security business. Together we examined what had to be done. When he heard what I wanted to do, he didn't want any part of it. I had to go it alone.

I rented a post office box in the next town under a phony name to get delivery of some small electronic parts. My second stop was New Jersey, the finest underground market for outlawed electronic merchandise on the East Coast.

I worked quietly in my garage, wondering if my invention would work. Testing was out of the question. I had a sign made up for the back window, one of those yellow and black ones that usually say, "Child on Board." Mine said, "Enter at Your Own Risk."

The gods were in a sporting mood, I guess. The car was stolen for the third time. I knew the police would recover the car in two days max if it was kids out for a good time. The pros, of course, would have it to a chop shop or to a Brooklyn pier for shipment to South America within 48 hours.

So I began the countdown.

On the third day, seventy-two hours later, there it was—a story in *The Daily News*, third page.

> "Brooklyn the scene of unusual assault device. Mysterious electronic blast paralyzes unidentified male driver on Pier 52. The Anti-Theft Crime Division reported an investigation in progress to locate the owner."

The article went on to report that police were puzzled by an unusual sensor installed below the airbag, which triggered the electronic blast.

I smiled. The good news was the damn thing worked. The bad news was the son of a bitch who stole it sued me for injuries.

Advice from a Lawyer

The divorce lawyer quietly listened without commenting. The story was all too familiar. Only the names changed.

The woman said she had a husband whose jealousy was unfounded. She was innocent, she declared. She had never been disloyal or given any cause for jealousy. She loved him.

She was, however, at her wit's end. He opened her mail. She had nothing to hide, but he said, "If you have nothing to hide, why shouldn't I open it?" He listened to her phone calls. He questioned her friends about her activities. Stress had become an unwelcome companion.

She felt sorry for him, but divorce seemed the only alternative. What would it cost? was her question.

The lawyer quickly appraised the situation. This was not a lucrative case.

They lived in a middle-class neighborhood. Her clothes were rather ordinary. She wore only a plain wedding band.

He made a quick decision. "I am going to do you a favor," he said. "I am not going to take your case right now. I will later, if you insist. Now, I want you to give some thought as to what more you can do to reduce his suspicions. Execute some unusual prank. Think of some unusual approach. Think out of the ordinary is my advice."

She thanked him and left with a thoughtful look on her face.

That evening at dinner she said to her husband, "Thelma called to thank you for the flowers."

"What flowers?"

"She said you would understand. I don't understand. Are you in love with her?"

"Are you crazy?!" he yelled. "I didn't send any flowers. I am going to call her."

Thelma hung up on him.

A few days later, the husband found his wife in the waiting room of his office.

"Why are you here?"

"I thought it would be nice to surprise you and have dinner together in town tonight."

"I can't," he said. "I am meeting clients."

"I understand," she said. She left and waited outside his office.

Unnoticed, she followed him to the restaurant and waited until he was seated with his clients before approaching him. She sat down as if she were invited and introduced herself to his clients as his wife. After that, she didn't speak at all. The dinner ended abruptly, and the clients left, insisting they had another meeting.

He was angry.

"What is the matter with you?" he demanded as they drove home.

"Tell me about Thelma."

She looked into her pocketbook and removed what appeared to be a receipt, which she waved in front of him.

"What is this hotel receipt? It says Mr. and Mrs. William Bensen for May 23rd."

"It wasn't me!" he shouted.

"Well, it wasn't me, either."

These events multiplied. She opened his mail. She listened in on his conversations.

She followed him to work. She followed him home.

The husband finished speaking. The lawyer had quietly listened without commenting. He recognized the name.

"I am going to do you a favor," he said. "I am not going to take your case right now. I want you to give some thought as to what you can do to reduce your wife's suspicions. Think of some unusual prank. Think of some unusual approach. Think out of the ordinary is my advice."

AIDS in South Boston

In our family of aunts, uncles, and cousins, we never talked about Christopher. His father, my cousin Angelo, was a good father. He just could not understand how one of his sons could be homosexual.

The "old school" culture lingered in Angelo. He suffered with the idea that somehow he had done something wrong. Perhaps his wife had done something wrong. Or was it God's way of punishing him for something?

Growing up in South Boston, we all had to be tough. Christopher was the toughest. Tall, well built, with a beautiful head of hair, he stood out everywhere—in the schoolyard, shopping in the A & P for his mother, and at the Friday night dances at St. Anselms. He didn't dance much, just quietly moved around and joked and made sure that the guys didn't get fresh with the girls in our family.

No one knew exactly how we came to understand that Christopher was different or why. We loved him so it didn't matter. He moved away from home when he graduated, not to go to college, but to go to work. It scandalized the family.

Christopher became a hairdresser. He trained in one of those schools advertised on television. He was, however, a natural in his field. His reputation grew and so did his income. Manhattan lured him away. He still came to all the graduations, the weddings, and the baptisms, to all that celebrated life. But, suddenly he was no longer one of us.

Now and then he would send us a picture of himself styling the hair of a celebrity. Angelo was proud of him. Christopher was making a lot of money. He invested carefully and put his parents' names on any deeds. His success was our success.

Then he got sick. At first no one put a name to it. His mother visited him often with bowls of homemade soup and handmade pasta, but he did not get better. He finally told his father the truth. They wept together.

"It's not your fault, Dad. Believe me, these things happen. Someday science will tell us why. I had to tell you, Dad, because Anthony will need your understanding now. Promise me you will understand him. Promise me."

My cousin Angelo withdrew from all of us. We didn't understand the reason. We just felt he was taking Christopher's sickness hard. The fear and shame that someone might find out the secret kept him a recluse.

Some of us, however, had figured out what was going on. We paid a visit to the chief medical officer of the hospital and made our case. The chief was one of us. We made him an offer he could not refuse.

When Christopher died, the death certificate clearly stated the cause of death was pneumonia.

It was the beginning of a pneumonia epidemic in South Boston.

The Computer Expert

Everything in the marriage was fine until the computer arrived.

It was almost like the child they never had. They even gave it a name. George.

Suddenly, the quiet romantic dinners stopped. Movie going became rare. They stopped seeing friends. The bickering started when they both wanted to use the computer at the same time. It became worse when the computer started to protest, almost as if it, too, was suffering from what was happening.

First came the blackout screen when they yelled at each other. Somehow, when they quieted, it quieted.

Then the icons started acting strangely. When he sat at the computer, he could not log on to his favorites, but when she sat at the computer, she got his favorites.

The cut-and-paste tool was totally uncooperative. Even the keyboard protested. Any attempts at writing were garbled.

They contemplated divorce to end the torture once and for all. But they couldn't. You can divide the furniture; you can divide the bank accounts. You cannot divide the computer.

They decided to try one last frantic call to the 800 number, which had begun to decline their calls. They wanted to make one last heartbreaking plea for help to bring relief. They were refused. The operator hung up on them.

In despair, the husband went to the basement to tidy up his tool bench, and the wife went to the sewing room to mend a skirt.

A few days later the doorbell rang. A taller-than-average man wearing a mask stood holding an umbrella and a bag of books on the threshold next to a large box.

"I am the Masked Computer Crusader," he said. "Just give

me the facts. Only the facts." They did. He listened.

"Okay," he said. "Show me George." They took him to the room where the computer was located. He brought his tools in. He asked them to leave and closed the door.

Strange noises were heard coming from the room—bangs, crashes, groans, and then whistling, sighing, and beeping. They stood by the door for hours not making a sound.

Then the door opened. A strange light shone through the doorway. It came from a second computer attached to George by a kind of life support system.

"This is Georgia," the Masked Computer Crusader said. "Treat her well, and she will treat you well."

Then, holding his bag of books, he opened his umbrella and, just like Mary Poppins, flew out of the door and up into the sky.

They gasped. They smiled at each other. They held hands looking at the marvel.

They decided they should call the 800 number and thank them. The operator told them they never sent anyone to fix their computer. Furthermore, they never heard of anyone called the Masked Computer Crusader and suggested that they stop drinking. The operator hung up on them again.

First Kiss

I still get a shiver when I think of the first time I heard his voice.

I was eighteen years old and sitting on a bench in Central Park waiting for my brother, who was coming to meet me. We had arranged to go home together. Suddenly, I noticed a lot of commotion. There were yells and whistles and people running all over the place.

I felt a hand on my shoulder and a voice behind me breathing hard. It was him.

He leaned close to my ear and spoke in a low tone.

"My name is Tony," he whispered. "Please, don't be scared. Can I just sit next to you like you know me? I am running from the cops. But I swear to you I didn't do anything. Please. You have to help me."

I was frightened. I wanted to run away, but I sat frozen on the bench. I swallowed hard and said sure. He came around and sat down. He wrapped his arm around my shoulder in a casual style.

Without moving, in a tight tense voice I asked, "What did you do, rob a bank?"

"Hey, you were there?" he said, laughing. "Look, ever been in the wrong place at the wrong time? That's what happened to me. Honest, you have to trust me. I am not a bad guy. By the way, why is such a good looking blonde like you sitting alone in Central Park?"

I blushed.

"I'm waiting for my brother. He works near here. We'll walk home together when he gets off work soon."

Abruptly, he smothered me in an embrace, and I heard running feet rush past. I could feel his heart pounding next to mine. I couldn't breathe.

"Sorry," he said. "It had to look real, right? So, what's your name?"

"Esmeralda."

"You're kidding me, right? No one has a name like that and a face like yours. You look like that pop star. What's her name? You know the one."

I blushed again.

It got quiet.

"Life's weird, you know?" he continued. "One day you're in jail, and the next day you're on parole sitting on a park bench with a gorgeous blonde. I'm trying to get my life together, but the cops won't give me a chance. You come to the park often?"

"No, just sometimes."

Slowly, he got up. "I have to go now. Thanks a lot for giving me a break. Maybe I'll see you around." He bent and kissed me on the lips. Then he was gone.

I was wearing a fancy pair of dark sunglasses. He didn't realize that I was blind.

Fortunetelling, Greek Style

My mother used to read the past and the future in coffee cups. Well, what she read were the "messages" left by the coffee grounds on the bottom and sides of the cup after it had been tipped. The coffee was called Turkish back then. It was thick and syrupy.

Like the men who roamed the streets offering to sharpen knives for a dime, in those days gypsies roamed our part of town and told fortunes. They liked my mother and taught her well. She was usually on the mark with the answers to questions like "Will I marry?" "Will I get rich?" or "Will a love affair end?" Some of her friends called her a gypsy. My father didn't believe in that stuff. He never asked her for a reading.

I was 14 years old when a close family friend, Costas, died. After the cemetery service, we had all gathered at the home of the deceased for the traditional wine and Turkish coffee. Someone said to my mother, "Come on, Cassiani, read our cups." She agreed. Everyone drank up and very carefully turned their cups over into the saucer for the little remaining liquid to pour out.

My cousin Xanthippe was first. My mother glanced at the cup and said, "Xanthippe, you will be married soon." Xanthippe blushed. She was not exactly a groom's idea of a bride. She was built like a wrestler and ate like one, too. My mother read Chrysanthe's cup next, telling her that she would be pregnant soon, and it would be a boy. Chrysanthe's husband beamed. They had been trying to have a child for awhile. The readings lightened up the somber atmosphere.

Myrto, Costas's daughter, was next. As my mother looked into the cup, she drew a sharp breath and gasped. We all saw her reaction. "What did you see?" we demanded.

After a few seconds, she looked around and said, "We

will all gather here again in seven days." She would not say another word.

Eleni, Costas's widow, died in an automobile accident a few days later. The same people gathered again for wine and Turkish coffee after the cemetery service. When they asked my mother to read the cups, she vowed she would never do it again.

Time passed. Xanthippe did marry. He was a big man who owned a diner in Philadelphia. Chrysanthe did have a baby. It was a boy.

I was 25 when I asked her to read my cup again. She refused at first, but I kept insisting. I had met this guy, Thomas, who was sexy and interesting. We were having a good time and saw a lot of each other. I really liked him. He had not called in awhile, and I was worried.

I finished sipping my Turkish coffee and slowly turned the cup upside down into the saucer and waited. My mother picked up the cup, turning it over. Suddenly she dropped it, as if it had burned her hand. The cup fell and smashed on the floor. She claimed she did not have time to see anything. I knew better. Something was wrong.

I called Thomas and told him I wouldn't see him again. Our relationship had no future. He protested, explained his absence, and, taking a deep breath, declared he loved me. He proposed over the phone. I didn't know then that I was pregnant. My mother, the gypsy, did.

With Malice Toward Some

Ready. Set. Gone.

A friend introduced me to Speed Dating. "Stephanie," she said, "you can't imagine the opportunities." Speed Dating is calculated frenzy. Twenty men and twenty women sit across from one another. The women stay put. The men move along the chairs every four minutes to the next woman. Registration is $35.

I sit down and wait for the bell that times the interviews. Ready. Set. Go.

This guy starts talking a mile a minute. It is as if he won't have enough time. He rapidly says, "My name is Michael. I love my mother. I vote Republican. I have a dog. I have twelve payments left on my car loan. And I bathe regularly."

My turn. "My name is Gwen. I love my mother. I vote Independent. I hate dogs. I bathe regularly. I recently received a small inheritance."

Silence.

Time's up.

He moves to the next chair, and another guy is now sitting across from me.

Ready. Set. Go.

The guy stammers and sweats. "My name is Peter. I was born on September 23, 1960. I am a Libra. I like to dance and eat good food. My favorite book is *Steadman's Mathematic Principles*. I commute to work."

My turn. "My name is Susan. I love my mother. I hate dogs. I don't vote. I failed algebra in college. I am a Scorpio. Our signs are not compatible."

Silence.

Time's up.

The next guy just looks at me.

Ready. Set. Go.

I am waiting for him to speak. He doesn't. So I begin.

"My name is—"

"Don't tell me," he says.

"Okay, I am five-foot-two, 120 pounds. I am 42 years old. I love old movies and new clothes. I am getting some nice vibrations looking at you. I want you to know that I believe we can make this thing work. I like surprises. I hate sad endings. I cannot tell if the butler did it. I am a Gemini with Sagittarius rising, and if we have a one night stand I won't mind."

Time's up.

He didn't get a chance to say a word.

Now, sitting across from me, I look into a pair of warm, dark brown eyes.

Ready. Set. Go.

"My name is Robert. What is yours?"

I take a deep breath. "My name is Stephanie."

"I like that," he says. "What do you do, Stephanie?"

"I do graphics for the Now You See It, Now You Don't Company. It's been around a long time. There are 15 employees, and we pretty much behave like a family. A takeover bid failed recently, so I am feeling better these days. I like the job. I don't go home tired or out of sorts. I enjoy book reviews more than the books, and my favorite dessert is crème brûlée with a touch of ginger."

A few seconds pass.

Time's up.

The warm, dark brown eyes get up.

A husky voice says, "It is only fair to tell you that since I didn't hear the word 'you' from your side of the table in four minutes, I am not interested."

Ready. Set. Gone.

Just Another Bachelor Party

As the best man, the bachelor party was Harry's responsibility. Remembering his own bachelor party, he was determined to be original. He didn't know when the idea had taken hold, but the more he thought about it, the more appealing it became. The guys would ante up twenty bucks or more if the ad he found delivered.

The ad in *The Village Voice* promised satisfaction or your money back. You provide the party, and they provide the girls.

Getting the *Village Voice* girls to the party way up in Westchester was the problem. The party had to be somewhere private. The bridesmaids and other women had to be kept in the dark.

Sure, it was all right for the girls to have their fun with the Chippendale boys at the club on 59th Street, watching the guys strut and gyrate. If a guy just looked admiringly at another woman, however, there was hell to pay.

So, what's the problem with a bachelor party? The women didn't get it. This was a rite of passage. This was the last chance for the groom to have a little legit fun. These girls knew how to show a guy a good time. The bachelorette party would be a sedate affair compared to this. The maid of honor tried like hell to get some information, any information. She didn't learn a thing.

The guys would meet at a bar on 8th Avenue. A van would transport them to Westchester. It would remain a private affair.

Harry decided to respond to the ad. Placing the call, he asked some questions.

"No," the voice said at the other end of the line, "you don't have to come in person to make the arrangements. Just give me your credit card number for the deposit and the particulars. If we have any questions, we will call you. Of course, we understand your health concerns and the privacy concerns. Our girls are special, sir, I assure you. Yes, going as far as Westchester is a bit unusual, but we understand the need for privacy. We are still in business because we are discreet. Yes, we can provide enough girls. Yes, all attractive. We know you will be satisfied."

Harry got to the hotel a little early to be sure everything would be in order. The boys arrived at about six o'clock, and the open bar was ready. At 7:30, a black stretch limo pulled into the parking lot. The girls spilled out, smoothing their dresses, and headed for the Surf and Turf Suite. There, as they entered, they slowly removed their coats and their scarves. Casually, they each selected a guy, introduced themselves, and, with some giggling, took off their high heels.

Harry watched, amused. The boys would be talking about this for years. Suddenly, he noticed a familiar perfume and a familiar hand on his shoulder.

"Hello, Harry," a familiar voice said, "still looking for a good time?" Harry turned slowly and saw his ex-wife.

With Malice Toward Some

Kidnapped

My wife begged me to cancel my trip. I couldn't. I had been waiting for months for a visa to Baghdad. There was an opportunity to work at an archeological dig site as a volunteer alongside Pierre Balmain.

I met Balmain, a curator of the Iraq Museum, at a fundraising event I attended in Detroit, which has a large Muslim population. Digging was my serious hobby.

Speaking French and Arabic had been the persuasive factor in getting the chance to dig. I had traveled a lot with my parents. My father was a career man in the Foreign Office of the State Department, and I picked up languages easily.

I had done some digging in Cairo, but the money ran out. No significant finds meant it was more difficult to get funding. The dig had to close.

The sudden arrival of the visa gave Balmain little time to find me accommodations. I ended up in the Sheraton for a few days. Since it was already hot the morning I arrived, I thought I better enjoy the air conditioning while I could.

I unpacked and showered. Then I wandered outside to find a bite to eat. A taxi line was outside the hotel. I got in the first one in line.

Suddenly, the driver locked the doors. He was silent when, in English, I demanded to know what he was after. A few blocks later, he picked up two young men who greeted him by name, Hassem. They began to converse in Arabic. The subject was my ransom. I felt like vomiting. I thought it best not to let them know I spoke Arabic.

I was taken to a house located in a courtyard, and they locked me in a sparsely furnished room. Hours later, a young woman brought me a plate of yogurt and couscous.

"Eat," she said in English.

"Who are you, and why are you doing this?" I yelled.

"The movement needs money. You are just a piece of baggage to us." Then she left.

I realized my wife was right. These were indeed dangerous times.

Hours later, the two men arrived with a camera.

I decided to gamble. In a sarcastic voice, I spoke to them in Arabic.

"Take a good picture. When Ahmed Habib in Basra sees it, you will hear from him. He will know that his secret plan to use me will be exposed." I knew Habib was a household name in the Muslim community from our newspapers in Detroit.

They paled.

Without giving them a chance to speak, I continued in the role I had chosen to play.

"I have been training in Detroit for three years. Do you know Sheik Omar from the Umm al-Qura Mosque? Do you know Mahmed Massoud who funnels money to groups like yours? He will want to know who you are and why you have taken this unauthorized action. His timetable has already been interrupted."

Then I swore at them with a filthy curse about a camel and their mother and demanded some decent food and water while they checked my story. I told them to hurry, as I was expected at the American embassy for a briefing given to all Americans who want to do business in Iraq.

They looked at each other and, without speaking, quickly took me outside and shoved me into a tired-looking Mercedes. They drove silently to the Sheraton and let me out.

As I ran from the car, the first bombs of the invasion of Iraq began.

I am going to find another hobby.

Secrets

Women in our family kept secrets. They knew who had not paid the rent on time, who was pregnant before the father knew, and whose husband was fooling around. They never spoke to anyone about what they knew.

I had few friends outside the family. The family was a big one. Outsiders were not welcome. My cousin Toula was my best friend. We had no secrets from one another.

Toula and I got our first real jobs when we were 19. It was the year we got our own house keys. Our world started to expand, but we kept it separate from our Greek family life. We knew we had come of age. We could think for ourselves. We also knew our families would not understand, so we lived in two different worlds because we loved them.

I gave my first paycheck to my parents. And the second. Then I realized it was MY paycheck so I kept what I needed and surrendered the rest. Toula could not. Her father did not have steady work. Her mother, my Aunt Vasso, was sick a lot. Toula and her younger sister and brother had to take care of her. They didn't have time for fun.

I was 20 when I learned my first secret. I had bought a special dress. It was kind of daring. I went to Toula's house to show her. She answered the door, and at that moment, my Aunt Vasso ran by. I saw her face. Bruised and swollen.

A black eye. Aunt Vasso ran upstairs trying to cover her face with her hands.

Toula took me to the kitchen. "Promise," she said, crying, "you will never tell what you saw. Promise."

"I promise," I told her, "I promise."

"My father is a good man," she said, "but he drinks. My mother would be shamed if her family or anyone else knew."

"Don't worry, Toula," I said, hugging her. "I will never

tell anyone, not even my mother."

We didn't see each other much after that. Shame kept her at a distance. I would see her at church or the supermarket. She had changed. She was thinner, with a face that had hardened. She didn't smile very much anymore.

A few months later my mother called me at work and told me to come home right away. Toula's father had died after falling down the stairs. I wondered if my mother knew he drank. I hurried home because I knew Toula would need comforting.

The funeral didn't take long. The priest made the customary "He was a good husband and father" speech. Later, after the trip to the cemetery, the family gathered at Aunt Vasso's house for coffee and wine. My aunt, dressed in black, seemed relaxed. Why not? That part of her life would be easier now.

"How are you, Angie?" she asked.

"Okay," I told her. "How are you doing, Aunt Vasso?"

"You are a good girl, Angie. You kept my secret. I will tell you another. I pushed him down the stairs."

Take My Wife

I was tired of keeping house. It was dull, dumb, and never-ending. I had tried cleaning women like most of my friends, but they needed constant supervision.

Then I saw this ad in the local paper:

Take My Wife
Now you can have all the advantages of a wife
with none of the nagging.
"Take My Wife" does everything you want a wife to do
that yours doesn't have time for.
Call for a free estimate.

So I called.

A man answered, "Take My Wife. How can I help you?"

"I saw your ad and would like some information."

"Sure."

"Just what does your wife do that is different?"

"She looks your house over and tells you what has to be done and does it. She does detail work like cleaning the closets, which are always overcrowded. Or updating the medicine cabinet. I bet you have cough syrup that is too old to be effective. She can redo your address book, which is probably in tatters. Of course, she also does windows and regular stuff."

"How much does she charge?"

"She negotiates a flat fee at the time of the interview."

"Okay," I said. An appointment was made for the following week.

I thought I would see a large woman with big hands and a quarterback's body. I was in for a surprise. A petite brunette arrived at my door. I showed her around.

"Well," she said in a soft drawl, "you really need help. How long have those faded silk flowers been there? Your bookcase is a mess. You probably have been meaning to straighten it out, right? And the sneakers you are wearing need laundering. Can't keep your sink empty, I see."

I smiled and said, "Your husband is certainly a lucky guy."

"Really? Why?"

"You must do all those things at home right?"

"No, I don't. He is too much a perfectionist. He created the business after he trained me. And I was glad to get out of the house. So, do you want my service?"

"I certainly do! What will it cost?"

"Let me whisper it to you." She did, and I laughed out loud and agreed that she should begin immediately.

I had to admit she was worth the money. She cleaned the freezer without being told and restacked the food, labeling it properly. She selected the clothes that needed dry cleaning.

We ended up having a cup of coffee like old friends when she finished her day. I made appointments for the future.

After a while, I gave her a key so she could just come and go without my having to be home.

One day she came and said she didn't want to leave. What was I to do?

I called her husband and told him to change his ad. I would take his wife. Permanently.

Taken to the Cleaners

My friends call me Sam. But I call myself a jerk. Sure, I'll tell you why. You guessed it, the opposite sex. What they call the "Men are from Mars and Women are from Venus" problem.

The beautiful part is getting married. It is divorce that is ugly. Getting married is cheap in spite of the cost of the wedding. Getting a divorce is expensive.

You want to know how in hell could I miss the signals? I don't know how.

It wasn't like that in the beginning. We met at Barnes and Noble reaching for the same book. Seemed we shared the same passion—boat building. A cup of coffee later and we felt like kindred spirits. We met again at the annual boat show at the Coliseum and began to date. I tell you, friend, I could do no wrong. The dates were great. Sometimes I got lucky, you know what I mean? Very lucky. Hey, I am 46.

We gave each other surprise presents. Of course, mine were more expensive. We bought each other books. We challenged each other to find the most interesting and obscure restaurants and hideaways. It was never dull. I was anxious to set the wedding date, but you know the routine. The families have to meet. Then, you gotta meet the girlfriends and the boyfriends. So, we arranged a dinner, the one we called the "What do they see in each other?" meeting. Didn't matter what they thought. I was hooked. I had proposed, and the pearly gates opened. Marriage is a magic word for women, right?

Things were terrific until my friends started to suggest a prenuptial agreement. The subtle implication that "I trust you, but just in case, sign here, darling" may have caused a problem. Who knows? That's why I turned the prenuptial signing into a party and then tore up the papers. My lawyer was ticked off.

So why did the marriage turn sour? Beats me. It wasn't the money, because I had plenty.

All I know is that the magic moments were going to someone else. There were too many late dinners, too many wrong numbers, and I didn't get lucky too often.

Now I just wanted out fast. That's what I told my lawyer.

"So what is it going to cost me?" I asked.

"Everything."

"Everything?"

"Everything."

What the hell? So I am stuck with alimony. It's worth it.

"Where do I put my Samantha Livingston signature?"

The Anniversary Club for Men Only

The Club started as a joke. The bored husbands decided to observe their wedding anniversaries with a night out.

The purpose of the Club was to talk about *the* anniversary and what each of them did to make the anniversary celebration less boring.

Each was sworn to secrecy. They would share strategies. The women would never know. They would just see this as another night out with the boys.

John, with a record of 43 years married, hosted the first meeting at a restaurant. He confessed to a standard celebration. He brought her flowers. He took her to dinner. He purchased an expensive gift. She did not have a headache. He swore he would have preferred her to have a headache. Everyone laughed. At 43 years, no one expected anything different.

Some months later, Tom, with 20 years to his credit, was the next to host the anniversary dinner. He chose a bar. He confessed to a series of moves he thought were creative. He had hired a stretch limo to take them to the Vinoy for dinner. Unfortunately, he had to pay overtime because his wife was not ready on time. He had pre-ordered a fancy lobster dish with champagne, and she got an instant rash. They had to cancel the room reservations. She had a terrible headache. She wanted to go home. The evening was a disaster. Everyone laughed.

The celebrations continued. More husbands joined, and each tried to outdo the others with creative approaches to the anniversary celebrations. The stories, however, remained essentially the same.

That is, until one day it was the turn of a new member. He was celebrating his fourth anniversary. He hosted the affair at a disco club and laid out the strategy that made this anniversary memorable.

First, he told the group he had lied to his wife. He told his wife he would be out of town and could not observe it on *the* day. She cried with disappointment. A few days later he told her he was able to make arrangements to be together just two days after *the* date. She cried some more. Finally, he told her he was able to celebrate on *the* date. She was thrilled.

The day arrived. She bought him a handsome, expensive briefcase. She prepared a sumptuous dinner complete with candles and flowers. She then appeared in a revealing nightgown. Of course, he told the men, he was expecting a come-on. After all, it was their anniversary. Most women add a little more sparkle to an anniversary celebration. He was prepared.

Sorry, he'd said, but he had a terrible headache.

"What can I do to make you feel better?" she asked. He whispered in her ear. She was shocked.

But, she didn't say no. She would try it. But he must promise never to tell anyone what he asked her to do. He promised. He lied.

The Assignment

My editor wanted a new human-interest series for our local newspaper. "Think outside of the box," he said.

He wanted me to go beyond the usual "Neighbor Rescues Cat from Pool" or "Widow Helped by Local High School Fundraiser."

I thought about it for awhile. I realized that the challenge affected my job. I had to produce with some originality.

I wanted to produce. I also wanted to impress him.

"What if," I started asking myself, "I made an unusual survey?" This led me to the civil registrar's office. A tired looking elderly clerk mentioned the old records in the basement. Records that were musty and dusty and forgotten. The ones they never got around to putting into the computer because the money ran out.

The basement was dark and poorly ventilated. Bulging boxes were stacked against a wall.

One box was coming apart at the seam. It had been duct-taped to avoid being spilled accidentally. I opened it and found it contained the names of civil marriages that had taken place on June 4, 1955. June brides. How did these marriages stack up to today's statistics? My "what if" started to take shape. What if they were still married? What if some had divorced? What if some had died?

I started with the first folder. John Gable and Irene Graybar. "Hmm," I thought, "at least the monogrammed initials remained the same on the linen towels if they divorced." The next folder was Michael Damion and Carol Grange.

And so on. I copied info on about 14 marriages when a name I recognized popped up.

Robert Merrill and Janet James. Robert Merrill is my father's name. Janet James is not my mother. A coincidence?

I took a deep breath. My "what if" had become scary.

The address listed in the 1955 registry was not my father's.

For the hell of it, I decided to go to the address. "Part of my research," I told myself. "Relax." The house was in a middle-class neighborhood. I rang the bell. A pimpled, rumpled teenager answered.

"Is Mr. Merrill home?"

"Who?"

"Mr. Merrill."

"Never heard of him. Sorry."

"Is Janet James home?"

"Who wants to know?"

Thinking quickly, I said, "I am planning the reunion of the graduating class of 1945. Is she home?"

"You're out of luck. She's dead. We rented the house a long time ago. Her lawyer is managing the property now."

I thanked him and left. The "what if" factor had revealed another coincidence. My father is a lawyer.

I distracted myself by working on the other names. Some were in the phone book. Others were not. Of those in the phone book, some were dead. Others divorced. I know you want statistics, but, listen, I had a hard time concentrating.

I decided to question my father. "Who was Janet James?"

For a moment he seemed perplexed. Then, shoulders sagging, he sat down. "Janet James was my first wife. I was 21 when we married.

"We divorced very soon after. Later, when I met your mother, I decided not to tell her. Her parents would not have allowed her to marry a divorced man."

I hugged him and said his secret was safe.

I started a "what if" column. My first column posed the question: "What if your father had a secret marriage before you were born? Would you tell your mother?"

The response was overwhelming.

My editor was happy.

The Backgammon Club

Anne did not like being divorced. Her husband, Gus, didn't like delivering the alimony, but this was part of the agreement. Anne was bitter. She had lost him to a younger woman.

He wanted to remarry but could not afford it. How long would Carla wait for him? "If only Anne would remarry," he thought.

Gus reviewed the situation calmly. Identify the problem. Fix the problem.

Problem #1: Where were the best opportunities to meet men with money?

Problem #2: How to keep his part in the scheme a secret.

He reviewed the social clubs in the area and selected a private backgammon club in the next town. Speaking to the membership chairman, in confidence, he simply said, "Man to man, I need a favor. My ex-wife won't leave me alone. I have to get her off my back. Maybe if she learns this game and meets new people she can make a life for herself."

The membership chairman was sympathetic. He was a divorced man and recognized a universal problem. The Ex-Wife. He accepted the payment for the membership dues, personally filling in the application and sponsoring Anne himself.

The following month, while delivering the alimony check, Anne told him she accepted an invitation to join a backgammon club even though she didn't know how to play. They would teach her.

"What's the club like?"

"Nice. It is quite big. The game is kind of strange. I am at the beginner's level. The stakes are very low."

"They play for money?" Gus asked, surprised.

"No. They have some kind of system where you exchange

favors instead of money if you lose a certain amount of games."

"What kind of favors?"

"Well, once I had to cook dinner for five people as a favor to the winner. Another time I had to carry the winner's golf clubs at a tournament. It's a lot more fun than winning money. They tell me I am getting to be good. I go to the next level of play if I don't lose any games."

Gus dropped the conversation.

Some weeks later, Anne announced she had moved to the intermediate level at the backgammon club and the stakes were higher.

"What does that mean?" asked Gus.

"I was told it wasn't sporting to ask, so I don't. I am learning to play with the cube. My game is improving all the time. I just won a big tournament. I asked for an interesting favor."

"What favor?"

"Just for fun, I asked my losing opponent to follow Carla and tell me what she does. Did you know, Gus, that you're not the only man in her life?"

Gus paled. Cursing her, he left quickly.

The following month, Anne had no time to chat with Gus.

"Just slide the check under the door," she told him on the telephone. "I have to practice strategies because I am quickly moving to the next stage."

Anne soon reached the most advanced level. Her skill and coolness were the envy of many of the members.

Gus found himself dreading the monthly delivery of the alimony check.

At last, Anne announced to Gus that she had won big. She had won very big. The losing opponent was wealthy and single.

"I think he lost on purpose," said Anne. "He wants to marry me, but I told him I needed a big favor first. I want him to get rid of Carla."

The Birth Certificate

"Hello? Is this Martin McCauley? This is Mathew Connors. I am your son."

I hung up. What kind of crap was this?

The phone rang again.

"Hello?"

"Don't hang up. I don't blame you for being suspicious, but you were married to my mother, Ethel Goodman."

I didn't hang up. I sat down.

"Listen, I know how you feel, because for days I couldn't get it together after I found out."

I couldn't speak. Ethel Goodman walked out on me 37 years ago.

The voice continued. "I found out by accident when I was going through her papers after she died. I saw that the name on my birth certificate was not the same as my father's. He died a long time ago."

"What is your name again?" I asked.

"Mathew Connors."

"Are you married?"

"Yes, I have two children. You have two grandchildren. I would like to meet you."

I was silent.

"I know this is kind of rough, but I think it would be good if we meet. I have some free time next month if that's okay."

I paused and then said, "Listen, call me again. I have to think about this."

"Sure. I understand. Good-bye."

The phone line went dead.

Ethel Goodman. The past assaulted the present. I didn't like it. We had been married for about three years when she walked out on me.

"Time's up," she'd said. Just like that. As if she had

dropped in for a visit and suddenly remembered she left the oven on or the car running.

"Listen, Martin. It already lasted longer than we thought it would. I can't keep trying forever. It is over. Get it? Over. The checkbook is in the drawer. I am not taking anything that belongs to you."

The divorce papers came soon after. I never saw her again. I didn't know what had happened to her. I didn't want to know.

I never remarried.

Now this phone call 37 years later.

A few days later a note with a picture arrived. It just said: This is your family. Mathew.

His arm was around his wife. She looked like a typical PTA mother. The two children were staring into the camera. A boy with his hands on a kite and a girl with a doll. Mathew was smiling and waving. A dog was at their feet. A swing hung from a large tree. A two-story frame house with a picket fence dominated the background.

I was ready when he called again.

"Hello Mathew. I am glad you called. I would like to see all of you. Let's get acquainted. It isn't every day that a man wakes up and finds out he has a son and daughter-in-law and grandchildren and a dog and a kite. You know what I mean?"

"Sure I know what you mean, Dad."

So, here I am at 62, waiting and willing to exchange my quiet life for a new one, a new life that doesn't really belong to me.

Hell, I am not going to tell him his mother left me because I couldn't have children.

The Bounty Hunter

After my father died, my mother did odd jobs to make a living. My mother is a woman who looks like a Sunday school teacher. She is petite and wears glasses. You wouldn't know to look at her that she is a bondsman and bounty hunter.

She works alone most of the time. When she is up against some big guy, she hires a couple of guerillas. My mother carries a Beretta, and her rifle is always in the trunk. Mom tried to train me, but I am not the type.

She fell into the bounty business by accident when the cops picked up Aunt Jane's husband. He was arrested for assault with a deadly weapon. Aunt Jane had a secret admirer who hadn't stayed a secret. But her husband was family, so my mother bailed him out. She guaranteed he would appear in court. He didn't. He skipped.

That's when she learned about the bounty business. For 10% of the bail set by a judge, a bondsman underwrites a defendant's release from jail. When a defendant skips, a bounty hunter is hired to find him. My mother was one of the few who became both bondsman and bounty hunter. She made a nice living—$200,000 in a good year. Twenty percent of felony defendants skip before trial. The bondsman gets to keep the bail money and any collateral if the defendant skips.

Mom was a natural bounty hunter. She knew how to operate. She caught Aunt Jane's husband with her Sunday school voice, low and sweet with a slight drawl. She was making inquiries about her poor baby brother who went missing without his medication.

My mother almost always got her target. She missed only once. It still annoys her when she thinks about it. The defendant's name was Roberta. She was tough. Her specialty was blackmailing men who were old enough to be her father.

Her trouble was that she started to freelance and picked the wrong guy. Horace Harding was the father of the local president of the Civic Association. It was a high profile case. One of the guys who had worked with Roberta put up the bail money. I guess he thought he could get Roberta back in the business. He put up a nice piece of change to get her out. She skipped.

My mother went after her with a simple routine. Roberta's name and social security number were posted on a special search website. Then my mother obtained Roberta's phone number. Roberta actually answered the phone. She hung up quickly, but she was not quick enough.

After punching a series of numbers into her phone, mom dialed a special 800 number used by private investigators and bounty hunters to find the address. Roberta was gone by the time my mother got there. The trail went cold. Roberta had been planning this for awhile.

Without telling my mother, I made some inquiries. I went to talk to one of the women still in jail who had shared the same cell with Roberta. I offered to pay her well if she would talk to me. She did. Roberta had saved enough money to get out of the business.

"You'll never catch Roberta," she said, smirking. "Roberta is now a Robert."

The Breakfast Club

The Breakfast Club started at the Century Diner, owned by John and Toula, in Stamford.

It wasn't really a club. The breakfast meetings started when George, who was retired, got divorced. Breakfast was a drag, so the diner became his morning habit. He met Dennis, a bachelor, at the diner counter early one morning. Dennis had a hangover. George suggested a raw egg cure. Costas, a widower on the other side of the counter, agreed. A widower with no children, Costas liked starting the day with people. He liked these guys and suggested they take a booth. Breakfast started to take more than just half an hour.

John wondered about this bunch. Here was a man with an ex-wife, a bachelor with no wife, and a man with a dead wife.

What they needed, John told his wife Toula, was a man with a wife. That would free the table quicker, because the married man would have to go home quicker.

John introduced Nick, who was married, to the group at the table. Nick started coming to the diner while his wife Rena was visiting her mother in California. The booth was filled.

The morning breakfasts started everyone's day with a pleasant tone.

However, the waitress soon complained about how long they kept the table, the cook complained that they ordered the same breakfast everyday, and the cashier complained about the constant mix-up of the checks. Nick's wife Rena, who had returned from her visit, complained that what started out as a temporary visit to the diner was now every day for Nick.

Seeing the problem as a challenge, Rena showed up at the diner for breakfast every day, too. But she sat at the counter. One day a woman sat down next to her and was crying. Ellie was newly divorced and could not stand having breakfast alone. Rena comforted her. On the other side of

Rena, at the counter, was Mary, a slim young woman new to the neighborhood, who was an exercise freak. She devoured eggs and steak and coffee every morning after a marathon run around Stamford's lake.

The three women decided to share a booth. It was then they all noticed the quiet gray haired woman who had a cup of coffee and dressed in black every day. They invited her to join them. She did. Eleni was a widow and, as such, missed taking care of a man. Cooking was no longer a pleasure.

Toula saw two tables losing money. This upset her.

"This is too much, you have to do something," she told her husband.

John asked both tables to help him with suggestions to increase business.

The women suggested that getting the men married would free up that table.

Then Toula had an idea. She would arrange a blind date breakfast on the house.

Costas the widower got the widow Eleni.

Dennis got the exercise freak Mary.

George got the newly divorced Ellie.

Toula told John she wanted to have breakfast with Nick, the married one, from now on.

"You're kidding," said John. "What about me?"

"You get Rena," said Toula.

The couples were ideally matched. They all lived happily ever after.

Rena persuaded John to sell the diner and move to Florida where she could keep an eye on him after he opened a new diner.

The Case of the Drunken Teenager

The judge could tell this was their first court appearance. The nervous mother glanced at her son, unable to shield him from the proceedings. The subdued father had his arm around the shoulders of the teenage defendant, a skinny blond kid of seventeen.

The charge—DUI: Driving Under the Influence.

To the ambitious prosecutor, this was just a routine "let's get 'em young to keep 'em off the streets" case. To the older defense attorney, assigned by the Legal Aid Society, it was a "how can we keep this kid from going under" kind of case.

Court was now in session. The prosecutor began.

The arresting officer was sworn in. He gave testimony as to the date and time of the arrest and detailed the property damage was estimated at about $1,500. The car had crashed into a newsstand and fire hydrant. He administered the sobriety test immediately. It registered off the charts.

The Legal Aid attorney put the defendant on the stand.

"Do you understand the charges brought against you?"

"Yes."

"Your name is Paul Kelly?"

"Yes."

"Can you describe the events that took place on October 27 of this year?"

"Yes sir. I was filling out my driver's license application and under the section that read, 'Are you known by any other name?' I put no."

"And then what happened?"

"My parents looked the application over before signing it. Then they said they had something to tell me. They told me I had another name. I had been adopted right after I was born in 1986."

"You had no idea until then that you were adopted?"

"No. Not a clue, man. Not a clue. It took me by surprise. I was shook up."

"Then what did you do?"

"I took my dad's keys from the hall table and went for a drive. I was upset. I stopped by my friend's house to tell him, and we had a few beers. Then a couple of drinks."

"And then?"

"I decided to go back home and talk to my folks. I felt like a jerk. I know they love me. I was just pissed. It was my birthday in a few days—October 30th—and I felt like I was tricked…dumb, I guess."

"How is your schoolwork?"

"Not bad. I made the Honors List a few times, and I have an application to the State University. My folks can't afford more."

"Are you working?"

"Yes. I am training as a mechanic at the garage in Spring Hills. I want to be an electronic engineer, but it takes a lot of money."

"How do you feel about drinking now?"

"It's a bummer. I was vomiting all over the place when the cops got me."

Legal Aid rested their case.

The judge looked at the parents. They stood next to their son, their arms around his thin shoulders. It was the judge's turn now to render a decision. Damages were to be paid.

The fine was suspended because this was a first offense. However, Paul Kelly would be on probation for one year. The probation visits would be coordinated into the judge's schedule. She would keep an eye on him.

Paul Kelly and his parents would never know, of course, that she had given him up for adoption on October 30, 1986.

Next case.

The Cemetery

He didn't realize that she was observing him at first. She saw him as he got out of a shiny BMW parked in the cemetery parkway. He walked slowly to one of the graves, newly created, paused, and then looked up. He saw a well-dressed attractive woman wrapped in a beaver coat sizing him up. She saw a well-tailored Armani suit.

"Like the car," she thought, "expensive but low key."

He acknowledged her quietly and then in a few minutes walked over and introduced himself.

"My name is Howard McMillan. Are you visiting someone here?"

"No. My name is Betsy Browser, and, actually, I am investigating burial sites for my parents. Are you visiting someone here?"

"My wife. Over there."

"Oh, my condolences."

"Have you found something suitable for your parents?"

"Not yet. I am new to this area. My parents are now staying in an assisted living residence. They are both in poor health. They thought it best to be prepared, so I am looking around."

"Would you like a cup of coffee," he asked, "to take away the chill today?"

"I don't know," she said hesitating. "Oh, I guess it's okay."

"Good. It is not my usual practice to pick up beautiful women in the cemetery."

Trying to make conversation at the diner, she asked, "Were you married a long time?"

"No. About a year and a half. It was my second marriage. You married?"

"Divorced."

"Oh, sorry about that. Any children?"

"No. Thank goodness."

"Well," he said, "goodness had nothing to do with it."

They both laughed.

They agreed to meet again for another cup of coffee in two weeks.

At their next meeting, she asked him what he did.

"This and that. I make money. You?"

"I do research for a small company here in town. Consolidated Services, Inc."

"Never heard of them. So, what do you do for fun besides hang around cemetery plots?" he asked.

"This and that," she replied playfully.

"Ah, a mysterious woman. Perhaps you will let me discuss this mystery over dinner."

Dinner led to the theater. The theater led to the art auctions and a gentle sparring about their professions. She talked investment strategy, and he talked fine dining.

Over drinks, she asked him if he had done any more of "this and that."

"I tried," he said, "but I am distracted. I may have to marry you to be able to focus again. Will you marry me?"

She was silent for a moment and then said, "I might marry you if you can explain why you purchased five plots on the same day, in different parts of the same cemetery, three of which are already occupied by your wives. Than, displaying a detective badge, she continued, "You are under arrest. You have the right to remain silent..."

The Charity Auction

It seemed like a good idea at the time. Fundraising had become difficult. Innovative approaches were needed. An idea occurred to Mrs. Grace Hollingswood III, who was chairperson of the event. She realized that an untapped market of single, successful, and sensual women existed.

Amanda, a tall lanky blonde with a successful travel agency, epitomized such a woman. As co-chair of the event, she enthusiastically endorsed the idea.

The idea—auction a dinner date with a bachelor. The women would be challenged, and the men would be flattered. The women would choose the restaurant and pick up the tab as well. If one was clever enough, dinner for two could be enjoyed in Paris. Grace would have to get her husband's help. Someone had to check out the bachelors to be certain they were single.

How to get the names? Ask the single, successful, and sensual women which men they would like to bid on. Naturally, the invitation to participate would not reveal how the names were obtained.

The idea generated a great deal of interest and curiosity. Names came pouring in. Pruning became necessary. Snapshots were made part of the acceptance package. An auctioneer of estate jewelry from the next town was delighted to accept an invitation to host the event.

The fundraising date arrived. The Yacht Club was filled to overflowing. Men and women alike were handsomely dressed. Excitement filled the spacious room. The bidding began.

Good-natured shouts and murmurs of each successful bid were matched only by the sizes of the bids. One bachelor fetched a high bid of $350.

Suddenly there was an awkward silence. The picture of Mr. Samuel Hollingswood III appeared. Grace, his wife, was stunned. This was a joke, right? The auctioneer proceeded.

"Who will bid for this charming man?"

Grace had to act fast. The mistake would be considered a planned joke. She opened the bid at $500.

Amanda, standing in the rear, raised her hand. "I bid $5,000."

With Malice Toward Some

The Day I Lost My Husband at Wal-Mart

Now, listen. I didn't try to lose him. I always asked him to go shopping with me, and he always said yes. You're thinking that my husband was like one of those men you always see sitting in a chair at Dillard's holding a woman's pocketbook with bags of merchandise around his feet, looking like he was having a gastric attack. Well, he wasn't that kind of man. He loved giving his opinion on anything I wanted to buy. Of course, we didn't really agree all the time.

He understood that I just loved to shop. Anytime. Anywhere.

That day, he said he didn't want to come with me, but I insisted because I knew deep down he really did want to join me. It wasn't such a big argument. He finally said yes.

Wal-Mart was very busy. You know how big it is. I just asked him to go to the housewares department with me to look at the deep fryers I saw on a cooking show.

Somehow we got separated. I didn't pay much attention because I knew he would find me. He always did. Well, I waited at the housewares department with my selection, but he didn't come. I went up and down the aisles looking. He wasn't at the gadget center or at the automotive section. I even checked the place where you can sit and have a cup of coffee to refresh you. He was not there.

I got desperate. I went to customer service and explained I had lost my husband. A bleached blonde standing in line behind me thought that was funny. "Do you want him back?" she asked, laughing.

"Something must have happened to him in the men's room. Would you check?" I asked frantically. My husband was not there.

"He must have left," the manager told me. "It happens all the time. Husbands just get tired. He will be back."

I went to the parking lot. The car was still there. I didn't have the keys. I went back to the manager.

"The car is still there," I told him. "He has to be here in Wal-Mart. He has to!"

So the manager went on the public announcement system and called his name. "Mr. Philip Wylie to customer service please."

I waited. And waited. I finally went home. No one could understand what happened. But I knew. He had been kidnapped! I waited to be contacted.

A few days later I got a telephone call from Fiji.

It was Philip. He said he was okay. He found a place where there were no Wal-Marts or malls. He was never coming back.

With Malice Toward Some

The Eye Operation

My husband brought me home from the hospital today. I am upstairs in our bedroom. I don't know what time of day it is. My eyes are still bandaged. I am simply glad to be home.

The doctors were pleased with the results of the operation on my retina. "Keep the bandages on," they said. "Rest, no heavy lifting, no stairs, that sort of thing."

"I can do this," I thought. The worst was finally over. All that time in the hospital wondering if I would ever see again was behind me.

I tried explaining to my husband what it has been like. "Put a bandana around your eyes. No cheating. Then try to get through one day without using your eyes. Rely only on your hearing and your sense of smell and touch. Maybe then you might understand how isolated I feel." He patted my hand instead.

So now I am following the doctor's orders. Resting. Still feeling the strain of the operation, I just want to sleep.

The phone rings downstairs. I still can't tell what time of day it is.

"Who is it?" I call out to my husband.

"Just Nellie. She wants to know if you need anything."

"Well, that is nice of her, considering how busy she is all the time. Tell her thanks. I'm okay." I hear some low-toned conversation and then silence. I drift off to sleep.

A few minutes later, the doorbells chime.

"It's just the dry cleaners," my husband calls from downstairs.

A strong aroma of coffee drifts into my room. "That's funny," I think. "Bill doesn't drink coffee."

I lower the volume of the CD player next to my bed, and I hear soft sounds through my doorway. I drift off again and am awakened by the sound of giggling from the kitchen.

"Who is here?" I think, and I feel for the little bell my husband placed next to our bed to call him. "No need to strain yourself yelling," he had said. I ring.

Moments later he appears.

"What's up?" he asks.

"Who is here, Bill?"

"Nellie's husband came by. We are having a cup of coffee."

"Well, I am going to sleep again…sorry, darling."

"Not to worry" was all I heard until I awoke to the sound of the TV downstairs. I ring the bell.

"Bill?"

"Yes, I am coming. How are you feeling now?"

"Awfully tired."

He comes to my side of the bed and sits down. I feel for his hand. It is hot and sweaty. Some unidentifiable smell hovers around him. I drift off again.

Later when I wake up, I try to reach the bathroom without Bill's help.

The house is still. I can hear the clock ticking. It must be very late.

Washing my hands, I feel his razor on the sink and smell the shaving cream and the cologne. "It must be morning, he shaved already."

"What time is it Bill?" I call out.

"4:30 in the afternoon," he says as he enters the bedroom.

"Anything you want?" he asks.

"Yes. I want you to tell me how long you and Nellie have been having an affair."

The Food Critic

The article in the *New York Times* read like an obituary, except that it was on the front page. "After 27 years of impressing clients and food critics alike with culinary creations like puff pastry filled with lobster and tiny artichokes, the legendary Le Chateau restaurant closed its doors. The police are investigating a shooting involving the world-renowned chef Maurice the Magnificent and Harold Muncher, the famous food critic and author."

Maurice the Magnificent, chef and owner of Le Chateau, had earned the Mobil Five Star rating three years in a row. His friend, the food critic Harold Muncher, had played a vital role in gaining recognition for Maurice. Harold's peers called him "the Cruncher." His savage review of a restaurant would send owners into hiding. Maurice, however, was culinary perfection in Harold's view. There was a table at Le Chateau that was always held for him. He was the consummate diner. As a food critic, his standards set the tone for many chefs. For Maurice, it had become a great burden to keep up with Harold's demands to create! Create!

The stress began to show on Maurice, who lost weight and became short tempered. He was constantly trying to create original dishes to meet Harold's demands and challenges.

His creations became famous. No one could duplicate the steamed chicken wrapped in lotus leaves. Rival chefs could not identify the secret ingredient in the miniature meatballs flavored with ginger and coconut milk baked in cabbage leaves.

The Cruncher's arrogance, however, knew no boundaries. His demand for partnership was overheard by a waiter one day.

"I can make things bad for you, Maurice. A few poor reviews properly placed and you will be history and so will your cherished Mobil Five Stars!"

A pale Maurice asked for a few days to think it over.

Harold continued to occupy his table. A series of spectacular dishes streamed to it. Braised rabbit with pumpkin slices flavored with laos, a rare Indonesian herb. Mahi-Mahi roasted in a delicate aioli sauce, followed by a special cake infused with olive oil.

Then, one night as Harold cracked snow crab shells for dipping into a champagne butter sauce, he stopped eating. A puzzled look spread over his face. He asked for a glass of '97 Chevalier Montrachet Madeira. He swallowed and paled. Abruptly, without finishing his meal, he got up and asked for his limo.

Harold left without saying another word.

No one saw him for a while after that except the doctor, who advised a bland diet and rest.

Two weeks later Harold emerged. Pale and thinner, he arrived at Le Chateau for dinner and sat at his usual table. Maurice hastened from the kitchen to greet him.

As Maurice approached the table, Harold pulled a pistol from his pocket and shot point blank. Maurice fell to the floor. He was seriously wounded but not dead.

The newspapers had a field day. Disappointed Diner Serves Disaster to the Chef.

Harold was charged with attempted murder. He confessed. His motive was revenge. A blood test had revealed botulism caused by a rare bacterial toxin whose sole source is the laos herb that flavored the pumpkin slices. The toxin, usually fatal, had deprived him of his sense of taste.

Maurice was then charged with attempted murder and also confessed.

Both Maurice and Harold are in Corning State Prison.

Maurice has been assigned to cook in the kitchen. Harold writes a food column in the prison newsletter.

With Malice Toward Some

The Fortuneteller

The voice in my head kept nagging at me to get a job. Any job. I found a curious ad in the local paper: "Do you like people? If so, we have a place for you. No experience necessary. Apply in person. Carnivals, Inc. Main and State Street."

"You are looking for a fortuneteller?" I asked in disbelief. "I don't know anything about fortunetelling."

"What's to know?" the carnival manager replied. "If they are single, tell them they will get married. If they are married, tell them one of the partners is thinking divorce. If they have children, tell them they have many problems, which do they want to discuss?" Take it or leave it was his attitude. I took it. The rent was overdue.

I arrived early on the first day for make-up and my costume. The prop guy supplied me with a rather pathetic gypsy outfit with bangles and bracelets and a half mask, which showed only my eyes. The crystal ball sat on the table. I was ready for business.

My first customer came around noon. A thin-lipped, nervous, skinny woman with no wedding ring. I took her hands. They were dry and coarse, with dirt under the nails. I waited for her question.

Not a word came. The boss was watching. I leaned forward. "I know why you are here," I said.

Taking a plunge, I told her that if she followed my instructions, she would meet the man she would marry in 48 hours. She gasped. She withdrew her hands.

"You will leave this place and go home and take a long hot bath. You will apply a small amount of fragrant hand lotion to your hands, and you will repeat these words ten times. 'My hands are ready to caress life. Who will be the lucky one?' Then you will go to Starbucks and order a cappuccino coffee at exactly 6 p.m. tonight and the next two nights. $5 please."

Next? An overweight, slightly bald fellow who needed a shave. No ring. I gave him the same advice. Another $5.

My strategy seemed to work. I sent all the singles to Starbucks.

The married customers were different. The married women needed to believe they were still desirable. The married men needed to believe that they were still frisky. My first married customer was in her early 50s. I took her hands. Maybe she was bored, I thought, or maybe her husband was fooling around. I took another plunge. I told her that her husband was waiting for a sign that she still loved him and found him interesting. If she followed my advice there would probably be no divorce.

"Go home, take a hot bath, but invite him to take it with you. He will no doubt be surprised. He may refuse, but tell him you won't ask him again, just this once. Tease him or challenge him, but get him into the tub. Have lots of bubbles. No candles. Wash his back. Admire his shoulders. Tell him how good you feel knowing that even though the years have changed, you still see him as he was when you first met. In a low voice, ask him to please wash your back. Be gentle, tell him, the way you were the first time. Then in a few minutes, tell him, 'Now be the tiger I know is in you.' $5 please."

Next. And so on. It was a long day. Tired and glad the day was over, I washed up and changed back into my own clothes. Starbucks was my next stop for a cup of coffee. It was crowded. I looked around. I saw a face I liked.

"Can I join you?" I asked. "I just want to sit with someone who looks as relaxed as you. You look as though you just stepped out of a long, hot relaxing bath."

"I did," came the reply. "Please join me. My name is Mark. What is yours?"

The Funeral

"Listen, Charlie," said the therapist, "these sessions are not working. I have a suggestion. Let's bury Diana."

"What are you saying?" I yelled. "She is not dead."

"The woman you married five years ago is dead," he said. "Diana wanted to live a storybook kind of life, promised by the deodorant ads, the whiter than bright smile ads, the Victoria's Secret ads. That woman is gone. She is not there anymore. You can no longer call out and say, 'Diana, I am home.' She won't answer."

I listened, stunned with this suggestion. This was the answer that 85 years of psychiatry could offer? Diana and I had been married about 4 years. I had come home after work as usual. Dinner was ready as usual.

"What kind of a day did you have?" I asked her.

"The usual," she said.

"What would you like to do after dinner?" We would usually watch TV or a movie. Maybe visit a friend.

"Get a divorce," she replied.

I couldn't think of anything to say. "Are you all right?" I asked her.

"No. I am not all right. I don't want to be married to you anymore."

"What have I done to you?" I yelled.

"Nothing. That's the problem."

"What are you doing to me?" I said with my teeth clenched.

"I am waking you up," she replied.

"What are you talking about?" I yelled again. "Haven't I worked hard, been faithful, given you everything you wanted?" I demanded.

"Yes, you have," Diana said. "I just believe that there must be more to marriage than keeping house, sleeping in your bed, having the whitest wash in town, or the newest car."

Just like that she left. Didn't take any money; didn't take many clothes. She handed me an address for her mail and left. Just like that.

"Well," said the therapist, "we have been all over that. You have to accept the fact that she is gone. That is why you have to have a funeral. Call it closure."

The doctor was right. I decided there would be a funeral. The death notice appeared in the obituary column of our local paper. It was a crazy thing to do, but I began to see the possibilities. The wake would be held in my home.

Naturally, everyone said I was crazy, so I had to explain.

"Listen up everyone," I said. "We are all here today to bury someone whom we all love. Someone who was okay. Someone who tried and failed and who is now in a better place. Someone I will miss, and I think you may, too. Someone who would not want us to grieve too long. Let's say a prayer for the old Charlie, and then let's party!"

Across town, Diana reread the obituary and smiled. It said that the deceased had been ill for a long time. The cause of death was boredom. She would ask Charlie's help in planning her own funeral.

The Gold Key Club

The message on the answering machine was clear. "Mrs. Reynolds, this is Officer Todd at the Clearwater Precinct Station. We found your husband wandering in the park, incoherent, and all we could get was his name and telephone number. Please bring any medication he needs with you."

"I must have gotten sloppy and missed the signals," she thought. Too much overtime and not enough sleep was her problem.

Sighing, she picked up the keys to the BMW and headed for the door. It would be a long drive.

She remembered the first time they met. She had received an elegant and mysterious invitation to a very private party six months ago. Attendance was limited to six guests. "Be prepared for something daring and different," she was told. Well, she certainly was ready. She had tired of the bar scene, the computer matching clubs, and the endless blind dates. She was on her way to becoming a recluse when the invitation arrived.

Intrigued, she decided to attend. "First impressions are important," she thought. "Better wear the Dior dress and the Cartier necklace."

She noticed him at once. Tall, blond, dressed in Armani. He smiled and introduced himself and offered her a glass of wine, saying simply, "Call me Robert." They talked for a long time, ignoring the others. She learned he was an only child drifting from relationship to relationship, looking for permanency. He could do most things well he said, smiling—like cook and clean. But she would have to find his real expertise on her own. If she wished.

She wished. They left as soon as she signed the confidentiality clause and gave her check of $1,000 as a donation.

In six months, she had become a new woman. She smiled at the cliché.

Life had become very interesting. Now this had to happen. What kind of explanation could she give to the police? How much did they notice?

"Play it by ear and don't panic," she thought to herself as she parked.

"I am Mrs. Reynolds," she said. "Is my husband all right?"

"Seems to be sleeping it off," the duty officer replied.

She was led to a cell in the rear of the station. There was Robert on a cot, sleeping.

"May I see him alone, officer?" she asked.

"Sure," he answered.

She approached the figure on the cot. Gently, she lifted his left arm and quickly and quietly inserted a gold key into a tiny opening and wound it steadily until it was taut.

"Hello," she heard. "Call me Robert. Would you like a glass of wine?"

With Malice Toward Some

The Health Freak

Fred started every day with a run around the park. Breakfast was always organic fruit and nuts.

He rode a bike to his job. He gave gift subscriptions of health magazines to his friends. He visited the gym daily after work. He was in great shape. Fred was also lonely.

Then he met Frieda at the park. She was not there to exercise. Her idea of exercise was walking to her car. Her car had broken down, and she was stuck. A somewhat large woman who loved her comforts, she simply opened the trunk of her car, removed a bag of potato chips and a folding chair, and placed it beside the car with the hood lifted.

Frieda saw Fred jogging toward her and waved him down with her bag of potato chips. She offered him some as she described her situation. He declined the chips.

"They will be the death of you," he said, and instantly regretted his remark.

Fred reached under the hood to fix the problem. It was an old car. A loose wire easily tightened.

"Give me a hand to get out of this chair," she said. Heaving herself up with his support, Fred suddenly realized here was someone who could really use his help.

"Have you ever thought of having dried fruit and nuts instead of potato chips?" he asked.

"No, why?"

Embarrassed that he might make her feel ashamed, he sputtered, "Well, they are good for you."

"Maybe, but you would be good for me. Can I thank you with a home-cooked meal?" She smiled at him.

"Sorry, I only eat organic," he said apologetically.

"Not a problem," she said, still smiling.

That is how Fred got less lonely. Gradually, he won her over to his health philosophy. She started to lose weight, bike with him on Saturdays, and gave up potato chips. He introduced her to his friends as his "good deed." Fred found himself feeling oddly affectionate toward her. She bloomed in his management of her lifestyle. Sure, she missed the potato chips, the fried oysters, and various pâtés, but life was a tradeoff, she reasoned. She liked Fred's attention.

One evening, Fred asked Frieda to meet him at the park, where he slipped a ring on her now narrow finger. He asked her to marry him. She smiled as she said yes.

Driving home that night, Frieda, contemplating a long healthy future, did not see the very large truck, which crashed into her very old car. Frieda died buried under tons of very good organic meat, fruits, and vegetables.

Fred was lonely again.

With Malice Toward Some

The Mourner

The funeral parlor was one of those sprawling multi-level affairs designed to accommodate more than one wake at a time. It looked like a catering hall from the entrance. The parking lot was hidden in the rear with a separate entrance.

The chapel viewing rooms were all occupied. The mourners were indistinguishable from one wake to the other. Ellen could have fit into any one of the five groups paying their last respects. She wore a fashionable black dress and a smart black hat that framed her fair skin and blond hair.

The wake for Marshall Buchanan was very crowded. There was no room to sit. The line for paying respects was very long. Ellen was not surprised. Marshall Buchanan had a very important son in the political circles of Washington, D.C. He had represented Ellen successfully in a civil suit. She was there to pay her respects to his father.

Ellen stood in the long line, which spilled outside the mourning chapel into an oversized reception area that served all the chapels.

Waiting for her turn, she realized the chapel next door was empty. The doors were open. An open casket was placed in the middle. There were no flowers. No mourners.

Ellen, very tired, left the slow moving line and went into the empty chapel, mechanically signing the register at the entrance. She sat down quietly in the rear of the empty chapel.

A few minutes later, a well-dressed man arrived. After greeting several mourners waiting outside the Buchanan chapel, he walked next door into the empty chapel. As he approached the casket to pay his respects, he saw Ellen. His face expressed surprise.

"A relative?" he asked.

"No," she said, embarrassed to offer the real explanation for her presence.

"Ah," he said, "a friend?"

"No," she said again.

"I see you prefer to remain anonymous."

She did not reply.

"I'm John Bailey, the attorney for the deceased." He looked rather startled as he spoke. "I am handling her estate."

Ellen did not speak.

She got up to leave, the lawyer watched as she departed. He observed her quietly greeting some of the mourners still waiting in line at the Buchanan chapel. Embarrassed to continue her conversation with him, Ellen simply returned to her car.

His client, the deceased, was an eccentric old woman who had outlived her husband, her children, her friends, and her relatives. There was no one left to mourn her but her lawyer. As a last mischievous gesture, she had added to her will that, though unlikely, if anyone appeared at her wake that person should receive half of her estate.

"And I believed I was going to get it all," thought the lawyer.

With Malice Toward Some

The Music Thief

I clean houses for a living. It's good money off the books. Some of my customers are really interesting people. I used to clean house every Thursday for Spice Boy George for years. He's famous, you know. He was really messy. Glasses and beer cans all over. Cigarette burns on the furniture. People were always calling him up or dropping in on him, begging him to listen to their music. I worked for his mama, too.

Last spring, I started cleaning house for a really nice older guy on Wednesdays. His name was William Johnson, a retired music teacher. Another customer of mine had recommended me to him. Mr. Johnson played the piano, composing music all the time. I really liked what I heard. I would hum some of the tunes while I worked. When I asked him if he was going to publish his music, he laughed. "I don't have the right connections, June," he said.

That's when I got the idea of showing his music to Spice Boy George. I didn't see any harm in trying to help. I just took a dozen or so of the music sheets that were spread around the piano. There were so many I didn't think he would miss them.

My regular day for Spice Boy George was the next day, Thursday. I took the music sheets home with me. He wasn't home that Thursday, so I left them on the piano. I cleaned up and put the key back under the mat. I planned on telling him when I went to work the next week that I had left the sheets there on the piano.

When I got home that night I found a message from my mama saying she needed me real bad and fast. I had to go to Alabama right away to take care of her. She had fallen and broken her hip. I notified my customers that I would be gone for a while. For those I couldn't reach, I left messages on their answering machines. In the meantime, I was so worried about my mama that I forgot about the sheet music I left at Spice Boy George's house.

I couldn't believe what happened next. I was listening to the radio in Alabama with my mama, and I heard some familiar music. It was Mr. Johnson's music. "He has finally gotten published," I thought. Then the DJ started talking about how this was Spice Boy George's latest hit, which was climbing the charts like crazy.

I quickly called Spice Boy George long distance. I told him what I had done and how I had forgotten about it. This was HIS music, he yelled at me. I was mistaken. Then he fired me and hung up.

Well, now I was really upset and ashamed. I called Mr. Johnson. I told him what I had done. I was very sorry. "No big deal," he said. "Thanks for the thought, June." He told me not to worry. A real gentleman I tell you.

The next thing I know, I am reading in the newspaper that Spice Boy George has been accused by the Wild Side Music Company of receiving stolen music and causing extreme mental anguish to the composer, their client, who could not be reached for an interview. A picture of the composer appeared next to the article. It was not a picture of Mr. Johnson. It was a picture of me.

With Malice Toward Some

The Neighbor Who Saw Too Many Movies

I am not a nosy neighbor. I mind my own business. But I couldn't help hearing the arguments next door. She was always screaming that she was going to kill him, or he was always screaming he was going to kill her. I was too ashamed to call the cops anonymously. I imagined the conversation: "A domestic dispute, right?" "Right." "Well, best keep out of it." So I did my best to ignore the neighbors.

One day, though, she rang my bell. She was a small woman. She asked if she could hide just for a few minutes. What could I do, say no? I let her in. Sure he came looking for her—but all I said was I had just come home, that I didn't know a thing.

Things got quiet for a while. Then they started up again, really loud and rough. I thought of going over to see if she was all right. I rang the bell. I would tell her my phone was dead and ask if she had a problem with theirs. It took a long time for the door to open. When she finally answered it, her hands were badly stained red and her blouse was stained, too. "Sorry I took so long. Can I help you?" she asked.

I caught my breath and said, "My phone is out of order. Is yours working? I want to call the phone company."

"No," she said, "my phone is out, too."

"Oh, okay, guess I will wait for service to be restored." I went back home and this time I called the cops.

"Listen," I told them, "my neighbors are having a bad argument, and I think something awful has happened. Her hands were stained bloody red and so was her blouse." I listened as the dispatcher told me they would send a car over. "Can you keep my name out of it, please?" I was assured they would.

I watched from the window as the police car with its flashing lights parked outside my neighbor's house. They went in somberly. They came out laughing.

"What's going on?" I wondered. I called the precinct.

"You're the person who called us earlier?"

"Yes," I said. "What happened?"

"Well, you were right. Her hands were badly stained red. Her blouse, too."

"Well?" I asked.

The cop laughed. "Your neighbor was cleaning a couple of pounds of beets when she answered the door. Her hands were still stained when we got there. She was using the garbage disposal, you know, cleaning up, when we checked out the house and the kitchen. Her husband was not home. You've been watching too many movies." I hung up.

Things were very quiet after that. I never saw him again. I saw her.

"How is your phone working?" she asked.

The Obituary

The death notice appeared in the usual manner on the back page but in unusual size. It was large. It attracted attention.

"Mrs. Demetrios Poulos died on February 12, 2003, after a long illness. A native of Greece, she had resided in Tarpon Springs since 1961. She is survived by her husband James Poulos. There will be a private viewing before she is returned to her native Greece for interment. In lieu of flowers, please send donations to your local Salvation Army location."

At the residence of Mr. James Poulos, the phone rang off the hook. Relatives and friends were shocked by the sudden death. "We didn't know she was ill," they all said. "How did Pauline die?" demanded the relatives and friends. "Why weren't we told she was ill?" they asked.

"She did not die," Mr. Poulos answered. "It is a terrible mistake."

"Mistake?"

"Some stupid misunderstanding. Pauline is alive and well. No, she can't come to the phone, she is very upset. Yes, I promise she will call you back."

Their sons were taking it well. Jim Jr., the oldest and a pharmacist, and his brothers, Daniel and Michael, thought it was better just to ignore it.

Jim Poulos, Sr., as he was now called, could not ignore it.

He decided to pay a quiet visit to the newspaper to talk to the person who took the ad.

Did they remember who placed it? "Yes, an older woman, plain." Anything unusual about her? "No, the ad was fully prepared. She paid cash and had a taxi waiting."

A visit to the taxi dispatch office and a twenty-dollar tip got him an address.

Half an hour later he found himself in front of a large

apartment building. Jim had not been here before. He found the super.

"I'm looking for my sister," he said. "Are there any older women in the building?"

"We have mostly Irish families here," the super said.

"Any Greek families?"

"Yes. As a matter of fact, a nice lady on the third floor, rear. She's not well," he paused, "walks with a cane."

Grimly, Jim got into the elevator. He rang the bell of the rear apartment. The door opened slowly. He gasped as he barely recognized the gaunt face. "Kalliope, is that you? You put that ad in the paper?"

"I wanted your attention, Demetri. It's been over 20 years since you walked out on me. Your divorce was not recognized by the church. I am still Mrs. Demetrios Poulos. I am dying, and I need to put my affairs in order. They include introducing you to the daughter you abandoned in search for a woman who would give you sons. Demetra. Come and meet your father."

The Ostrich Egg

Did you ever get a gift that was absolutely the most atrocious thing you ever saw? Eloise did. It was a wedding present.

You have to say thank you because the person giving it is a close relative or a friend of your mother's, and you don't want to hurt their feelings.

The worst offenses take place at weddings when the bridal registry is ignored. Eloise was registered at Bloomingdale's, Tiffany, Fortunoff, and Macy's. She thought it was safer to cover all her bases. It was not.

A unique wedding gift arrived by UPS. It could only be described charitably as a strange large white ostrich egg. Some artist put a fancy handmade mother of pearl beak on one end and ostrich feathers on the other end. The gift, obviously one of a kind, was wrapped beautifully and expensively. The card was written with a flourish: "Love always, M." A bold decorative M—Aunt Martha expected everyone to know who that was.

Most of us have an "Aunt Martha." Details like wedding registries bore her. She always gives something unusual and expensive. Sometimes the gift is outrageous. It is never dull.

Eloise's fiancé, a usually tolerant guy, took one look at the wedding gift and told her to get rid of it. So Eloise carefully put away the box and card until she could think of a way to get rid of it gracefully and quietly. This would be easy to do without hurting Aunt Martha's feelings. The newlyweds were setting up housekeeping in California. Aunt Martha would never know.

Where Eloise got the idea she could not remember. She was sorting through the closets and came across the old wedding gift, still handsomely boxed. Impulsively, she decided to send the gift anonymously to a name picked at random from their Manhattan phone book, which had moved along with everything else to their new California home. The name Genevieve LeClerc stood out. The address placed the residence in an upscale East Side neighborhood of Manhattan.

A visit to the post office and the deed was done.

Genevieve LeClerc was youngish at 56, still attractive, and with no shortages of suitors. She had simply decided to stay unmarried. Her friends considered her slightly aloof but excused it by attributing it to her European upbringing. She maintained her French accent and chic sense of style that was a plus in her profession as a translator with the United Nations.

A few days later Genevieve signed for the package. She exclaimed with pleasure at the contents. As she read the card that had remained forgotten in the box, Genevieve began to weep quietly. "Love always, M."

Maurice had not forgotten her after all these years.

The Poker Cure

Richard knew he had a serious gambling problem. Gamblers Anonymous did not help. Hypnosis was a waste of time. Therapy, a joke. He was desperate.

He heard, through the grapevine, of a secluded camp for addicted gamblers in Vermont. This institute did not advertise. Admission was difficult and only by recommendation of a previous client. Treatment was very expensive. No one discussed the treatment. An impressive 98% success rate was all he learned.

Methodically, he tracked down a former client by phone. Yes it worked, he was told. No, he was honor-bound not to discuss the treatment. If Richard were serious, and desperate, he would be recommended for an interview.

A few months later an opening became available. Richard was invited for an interview.

Dr. Harrington greeted him and discussed Richard's sincere desire to stop gambling.

"Let me summarize," said Dr Harrington, "so there are no misunderstandings. Once enrolled, you cannot leave without an official discharge. You will forfeit the $50,000 in escrow. Do you understand the rules?"

"Yes. Yes. What happens next?" Richard asked.

"A receptionist will show you to your room," replied Dr. Harrington. "Tonight, after a review of your medical coverage and the confidentiality contract, you will have dinner in your room. Tomorrow morning, after breakfast in your room, we will begin the treatment."

The next morning, promptly at 9:30, Richard was ushered into a bright, cheerful room filled with men playing cards.

"We would like to evaluate how you play poker," said the attendant.

"I was told not to bring any money," Richard said, breathing hard in anticipation of this treatment.

"That's okay," said the attendant. "We initially give you $1,000 in chips to evaluate your playing. Then we place you accordingly in the correct category at the institute."

Richard sat down and played a few hands. Wins and losses were about even. The other players did not speak. They were also under evaluation. He was moved from one table to another, winning some hands and losing others.

Suddenly, an attendant ushered him to another room to begin treatment. This room was entirely white. It was unfurnished except for one round table and six metal chairs, all of which were occupied save one. He could not believe playing poker was part of the treatment.

Each player had the same amount of chips. Pale and sweaty, no one spoke as Richard sat.

The game began. Richard won the first pot. The others—the losers—sat ramrod straight. A mild electric current surged through the metal chairs of the losers. Some drooled. Some sagged. Some gagged. All of them soiled themselves.

It was Richard's turn to deal.

The Scribe—21st Century Version

I am a computer freak. I live and breathe computers. Recently I was fired. "Downsized" is the word these days. Finding a job I like in the computer field has not been easy.

My parents are worried that I will never get married because all I want to do is sit at the computer. I don't date much. Most guys are dull. It worries me that some new software program will emerge, and I won't be able to get it first.

So I went to this job seminar. Their advice: Find a need and fill it. I decided to use my skills in another way until a job came along.

I went to the largest mall and rented a kiosk. I got a secondhand desk on which I put my computer and printer and posted a sign that read: "I Write Letters for People Who Don't Write Letters."

In the beginning, people just smiled when they passed my kiosk. My first customer was an old man with Parkinson's symptoms who asked me to write a letter for him to his grandson.

"Tell him about my adventures of living in a place where alligators are close by," he said. The old gentleman just sat in a chair and talked to me while I typed. I handed him a crisp addressed envelope with the finished job.

Word started to spread whenever someone sat in the chair. People gathered to listen to other people's mail. Some of it was not nice. I wrote a letter for a guy who was divorced and whose wife wouldn't let him see the kids. He just wanted them to know he would continue to try to see them. Some letters were just consumer complaint letters—toasters that did not work, refunds that never came, that kind of stuff.

Before long, I got to know a lot about the human condition. It depressed me sometimes. I wrote a letter to an attorney for a daughter who was left out of her father's will—his third wife had gotten it all. I wrote letters to the president asking for an invitation to the White House. I stayed very busy. Business started to pick up. Sometimes there were actually people waiting for me to come to work.

One day, a guy with a laptop appeared and said he needed a job. He had noticed how busy I was and wondered if he could work part-time. When he spoke of computers, it was as if he were describing a woman. Challenging. Interesting. Exasperating. Never dull in the right hands. I hired him.

Later, he asked me out. On our first date, he confessed that my parents had put an ad in the personals column that read: "Wanted: Single male, totally computer-oriented for challenging single female who is also totally computer-oriented. Professional as well as personal prospects. Must be interesting, exasperating, and never dull. Apply in person at the White Plains Mall."

The Shopping Mall

It looked like he was trying to pick her up when they accidentally met one day at the mall, that big one in Tampa with the Starbucks.

They were both just hanging out.

He knew when he saw her looking at the display in the window of Victoria's Secret that she would be a great date. She knew from the way he looked at her that she would have to be careful with this guy. They liked each other right away. He asked her if she could direct him to the food court. She replied, "I'll show you, but first I want to buy something from Victoria's Secret. Will you wait?"

"Of course!" he said. When she was ready, they walked and talked. It was nice.

"You coming back soon?" he asked.

"If you come," she said. So they started to meet at the food court and, after a while, finally had a date at the movie house across the road.

He told her who his favorite teams were. She told him about the books she liked. He told her about his family, making light that they came over on the Mayflower. She told him she was second generation Mexican American.

They knew that they had to meet secretly for a while. His family and her family would hold their ages against them. And worse, she let him pick her up. They would say she probably planned it.

The secrecy just added to their excitement. The mall was the perfect place to meet. It was big, and chances were few they would meet anyone they knew. It had everything. A food court, record stores, bookstores, clothing stores, and easy parking.

They didn't know who squealed on them. One day, his family abruptly showed up at the ice cream parlor in the food court. They called her a social climber and implied she was after the crown jewels. They grounded him for two weeks by taking his car keys. Then they told her family, and she had to hear "You can't be trusted" almost daily.

This didn't stop them. They had planned for this—can't take anything for granted, they had agreed. They had already filled out the marriage application. They had contacted the Unitarian preacher by phone to set the date as soon as the two weeks grounding ended.

"I don't see any problem," said the minister. It wasn't as if they needed permission from their parents. He was 75, and she was 72.

The Support Group

The ad was small in the local paper. Support Group for Rejected Lovers. Men Only. There was a telephone number, no name.

I had just broken up with my girlfriend. Actually, she rejected me. This was the second one. I couldn't understand this. I thought things were going so well. We had been together for a while.

Maybe I took some things for granted, but, hey, that's what men do. I think. Maybe I am thinking wrong. The ad appealed to me, so I called the number. A heavy masculine voice answered, very matter-of-fact.

"What's up, buddy?"

I fumbled with the answer.

"That's okay. That's why we are here. Come on down and let's talk about it."

I did. They met every week. The group was small; there were five of us. First names only. The presenter got things started by asking who wanted to begin. No answer.

"Okay. Raise your hands if you were rejected this week."

Three of us raised our hands.

"You first," he directed to a guy wearing glasses. "What did she tell you?"

"That things were not working out."

"What things?"

"I asked her that. She just said, 'You know.'"

"So," urged the presenter, "go on."

"So I thought things were okay. She said she wanted fireworks. I am a slow and steady guy. I'm not the type to look for fireworks. I don't know what happened."

Another voice piped up. "She found somebody else, you dumb bastard."

The guy sunk in his seat.

"Who's next?" asked the presenter. "You!"

The guy in the sweat suit answered. "Me?"

"Yeah, you. What happened?"

"We had been together for a couple of years. I noticed she didn't do the little things anymore, like hang up my clothes or wait to have dinner with me when I was working late. She was late coming home. I asked her what the matter was. She said we weren't going anywhere. I told her I thought we were doing fine. 'You are,' she said. 'I need to know where I will be six months from now. A year from now. I want marriage.' I never promised her marriage."

Then it was my turn.

"Well. What happened?"

I looked around. "I really don't know," I said.

Silence.

"Try again, buddy."

"Look. I don't belong here," I said. "I can handle this."

"Relax. Just talk. That's why you're here."

"Okay. She said she couldn't stand my being so possessive. I told her I just think she has too many other interests."

"Besides you, right?"

"Yes. All I asked for was just a little bit more of her time. She asked me if that meant marriage. I said no. So she left."

Silence.

"Okay, okay," began the presenter. "Let's have some approaches to the problems we heard. Who goes first?"

The first guy answered. "I am going to watch some late night Cinemax 'Skin'emax and see how fireworks are created."

The second guy cleared his throat and replied. "I am going to tell her that I don't want to be an aging bachelor looking for companionship. I am going to ask her to marry me."

Then it was my turn.

"I am going to start a support group called 'A Man's Perspective on Rejection. For Women Only.' I expect to be busy for quite a while."

The Tattoo

"The problem with my tattoo," George thought, "is that it needs explaining every time a woman sees it."
"Where did you get it done?" "Is it anyone I know?" "Are you sorry you have it?" "How much did it cost?"

He gave a different story each time. He was drunk. He had lost a bet. He was only 15.

It stood in the way of moving on in a relationship. If her name was Sally, she didn't like to shower with a tattoo named "Alice."

He had decided that he would neither pay the price nor endure the hours of pain that accompany its removal. Besides, there was no guarantee some part of it would not remain in the form of discolored tissue.

He decided the solution would be to find a girl named Alice. He would use the personal ads in the newspaper as a starting point.

The ad read: "Single, white middle-aged male seeks special lady named Alice to share love of hiking, music, good food, and sci-fi movies. No other names need respond. Enclose photo."

There were seven replies—four blondes, two brunettes, and one redhead. He was surprised to see that all of them were tastefully clothed.

He started with the redhead. He sent his picture and suggested meeting at the Fine Arts Museum. She agreed but asked where it was. He did not respond further.

The next choice was one of the blondes. He sent his picture and suggested meeting at the Fine Arts Museum. She agreed in her response. She declared DeKooning was one of her favorites. He did not respond further.

He responded to one of the brunettes next. He again sent his picture and suggested meeting at the Fine Arts Museum.

The reply was short. She had just been there, how about a change of pace? She named a local watering hole, the Lucky Night Bar, close to the museum. Interesting reply. He agreed.

They bumped into each other in the parking lot. She laughed and held out her hand, giving a firm handshake. "Lots of Harleys here," he said to start a conversation.

"Yes. There are."

Once inside, they sat in a booth observing the bar and ordered drinks and dinner. As the evening unfolded, they relaxed, getting acquainted.

Several dates later, he decided to disregard the other Alices. This one seemed okay. Soon Alice invited him to dinner. "Nothing formal," she said. "Come and meet my dog. I have a boxer named Luke. You need his approval to stay the night."

It was an invitation he was hoping to receive. That evening, the dinner went well. Luke seemed agreeable, sitting at his feet quietly. One thing led to another, and they ended up in the bedroom. He removed his shirt, and she saw his tattoo with the name Alice. She laughed as she removed her blouse. She moved toward him slowly. He saw her tattoo. A heart with an inscription that read: I Love Hannibal Lecter.

"Want to have some fun?" she asked.

The Violinist

I was amazed at her performance. She played the violin alternately like an angel, soft and ethereal, and then loud and vicious. Twirling lightly with her companion on stage, I wondered how she could do that and play so fantastically. I thought she was magical.

I first saw her perform downtown as part of a group that played on weekends at the fountain in the park, one of those cultural events the city is always sponsoring. Although they played a classical piece now and then, the music was mostly New Age. The band seemed to be plugged into every kind of black box available. Her figure was slim, and, when she played the violin, it seemed an extension of her graceful arms. She noticed me and smiled.

Encouraged, I introduced myself. "My friends call me Dennis. I'm in the accounting field. I know your name is Olga. It's a lovely name. You must like what you do a lot. I see you smiling all the time when you play," I said.

"Yes, I do. I have little energy left for anything else," she replied.

"How long do you rehearse?"

"Oh, three to four hours a day depending on the difficulty of the piece."

"What's your favorite piece? I like the Paganini the best."

"I like them all. They are all so challenging."

"Do you have time for a cup of coffee?"

"That would be very nice."

Soon, coffee together after her performance became routine. Dinner was added to the routine and then movies. Later, we settled into a comfortable pattern. I was content to hear her play, meet her at the back door of the stage, and then take her home.

One day I asked her to marry me.

She would like to, she said, but she was not prepared to give up performing. She felt I deserved someone who would put me first.

"Well, we both love your music," I said. "That's a good start."

She agreed to marry, but only after a trial run of living together.

We found a place that fit both our needs. I had room for the computer and printer and fax machines. She had a room soundproofed for all the electronic black boxes. Hoping for the best, we moved in together. I was quick to adapt to her routine of practicing and playing with the band. The occasional tour only made me miss her more.

It was on the return of just such a trip that I asked her to play for me. "Without the black boxes," I said. "We don't need that much sound, do we?"

"No, but we do need the turntable. I can't play the violin. I just play in sync with the music."

With Malice Toward Some

The Wedding Gown

The headline in the local paper blasted "Marvin and Melissa's Mismatched Marriage."
Now, the bridal gown of $15,000 hung at the Repeat Performance Resale Shop where Nancy found it.

It seemed made for her. Her fiancé Norman would like it, she was certain.

Her mother was very upset and superstitious. She pleaded with her to take it back. "How do you know what the history of this dress is?" she asked. "It might carry bad luck."

To humor her mother, Nancy went back to the Repeat Performance Resale Shop, apologizing to the sales clerk. She related her mother's fears and asked if they had any information on the bride. Sorry, she was told, all they knew was what they read in the newspaper. The bride never showed.

Nancy was now very curious. What happened to the bride?

The best man's name, Charles Suave, was in the wedding announcement. He agreed to meet Nancy when she told him she had purchased the wedding gown. Nancy confessed her dilemma about the wedding gown and her mother's superstitions. Charlie laughed out loud. Yes, he knew where Melissa was. She was with Marvin. She was angry at the circus atmosphere the expensive wedding generated and couldn't deal with it. It was not their wedding anymore but had become that of her parents, his parents, their friends, and obligations. Marvin understood and, though he was upset, he still wanted to marry her because he loved her.

"So what is holding up the wedding?" Nancy asked.

Melissa wanted to be married quietly in the same dress that she and Marvin had picked out. She had contacted the Resale Shop, but they did not have the identity of the buyer. Charlie was relieved to have received Nancy's call.

"Well, I am not giving up the dress," declared Nancy.

Charlie asked her if Norman would agree with her. "Absolutely," she replied. "We have the same values. I will even introduce you to Norman."

A few days later, Nancy introduced Norman to Charlie.

At the meeting, the men sized each other up, the way men do. Then they shook hands like old friends and started to talk about the wedding gown and women in general, laughing a great deal. They discovered they had a lot in common—they rooted for the same teams, played a poor game of golf, and had a passion for old black-and-white movies.

A few days later, they shared a couple of cold beers, and Norman invited Charlie to the wedding. Norman liked Charlie's smooth style and comfortable presence.

The duo became a trio. Nancy liked Charlie. He was charming and attentive and very attractive. When Norman was busy, Charlie stepped in to help run the errands. When Nancy was busy with wedding arrangements, Charlie stepped in to keep Norman company. Their other friends began to wonder if Charlie would be invited to the honeymoon.

The wedding day finally arrived. The bride's mother sat silent and unsmiling in the front pew.

The church murmurings stopped as the minister began the ceremony in the traditional manner: "We are gathered here, in the sight of God, to unite this man and this woman." In a bored tone, he continued slowly until, at the appropriate moment, the minister's voice rose as it asked the familiar question. "If anyone knows of any reason why these two should not be joined, let them speak now."

Charlie stood up and started to walk toward the altar with his arms outstretched.

"I object!" he shouted.

The headlines shouted "Norman & Nancy Nuptials Nixed."

The wedding dress went back to the Repeat Performance Resale Shop.

The Widows

There are too many widows. The widows outnumber the wives in my town. Some husbands believe in being kind to widows. Wives do not appreciate this unselfishness.

My husband John knew that I would soon be a widow. He always took good care of me. A practical man, he made generous provisions for my welfare. He also made me promise not to mourn him for too long. John didn't want me to be alone. He had a practical solution that shocked me.

"Read the obituary columns for the death notices of married women. Select one to attend as a friend of the dead woman. A new friend. Just sit quietly in the funeral parlor and listen to friends and family speak. You learn a lot about a person," he said, "especially the dead wife and new widower."

A few weeks after the funeral, I should show up at the widower's house and introduce myself again and return a book. I should express my sorrow that I didn't get to know her better. If something clicks for me, just make myself quietly useful and needed to the widower.

That's how I met my second husband, Mark.

Returning to a married status was great. My widowed friends were jealous. I wanted to share my secret with them, including Sara.

Sara didn't want to find another husband. She had had two already. Sara wanted to keep busy and make some money. She decided to start a club for widows. For a hefty fee, she would do the dirty work, like read the obituaries, select a target, and match a widow.

This worked well. She made money. Her business expanded. She computerized her operation and franchised locations in several adjoining counties. She was happy. The widows rejoined the married group. They were happy.

What happened next was not understood until much later. It breaks my heart that it happened to my widowed friend Charlotte.

Charlotte arrived at the funeral parlor to attend the wake of Mrs. William Bradshaw. Introducing herself to the widower as a new friend, she then quietly took a seat in the rear. A few minutes later, a woman sat down next to her. In a low savage voice, she said, "I know who you are and why you are here. You have some nerve. Get out of here now, or I will make a scene." Of course Charlotte left. Shocked and humiliated, no one saw her for a while, not even Sara.

When the local paper announced the nuptials of Mr. and Mrs. William Bradshaw and showed a picture of the couple, she surfaced. There was the woman who had verbally assaulted Charlotte. She was the new Mrs. Bradshaw.

The computer had made a mistake and sent two widows from the club to the same wake. One widow got a husband. One widow got a refund.

This Elevator Does Not Stop on the 11th Floor

"Hello? Paula?"

"Daniel!"

"Thank God you're home. Listen. I need your help. You have to take what I tell you to the newspapers. Tell them to come to the 11th floor of St. Elizabeth's Hospital. The sign says the elevator will not stop there. Just do as I tell you. Don't do what I did.

"You were recovering here when I visited you a couple of weeks ago after your knee surgery. I noticed a sign in the elevator that said, 'This elevator does not stop on the 11th floor.' I wondered why, when I knew there were 11 floors in the building. I counted them from the outside. Out of curiosity, I tried all the elevators. None of them stopped at the 11th floor.

"I did some snooping. I asked at the desk downstairs. The receptionist told me lies. She said there was no 11th floor. The cost of replacing the panel was expensive so they just put in a sign.

"I tried using the stairs but they stopped at the 10th floor. So I started hanging out at the hospital. I thought I had found a way to get to the roof from a fire escape. There was a door I assumed was a fire exit, but it was locked. I came back a few days later with a stolen master key and unlocked the door. I found myself inside a corridor that led to a small room that looked like a nurses' station. I figured I would just go and find the right elevator and prove to myself that this could be done, and then I would leave. I didn't get far.

"There was a dolly with several trays outside a door with a red light. I tried the door, and it easily swung open. I went in. It was a ward with a single long row of beds. Drooling men with vacant eyes occupied the beds.

"I got scared and turned to leave. A guard in a strange suit and mask blocked my exit. He was very angry. He marched me to the nurses' station where he made a call. Then he dragged me to a sterile room. Another attendant, dressed like an astronaut, took me by the hand. He told me to relax and then jabbed me with a needle. When I woke up, I was in that same room with those men on one of the beds. I pounded on the door. The guard swung his stick at me. I fell to the ground. 'You are stuck here,' he said to me. 'You've been exposed to an unidentified highly contagious and fatal virus. The public has not been informed so as to avoid panic.'

"Paula, I can't stay on the phone. They will discover I am missing from my bed. Call the newspapers. Help me, Paula! Paula? Are you there?"

"We are sorry. Your call cannot be completed as dialed. Please hang up and try again."

Valentine's Day Massacre

My boss, Ernie, should never have fired me. I had been working in his florist shop for 12 years. I never cheated him, and I always gave him an honest day's work.

So what was his problem? His wife Helen and his girlfriend Heidi were away at the same time. He wanted to get a little action from me. I am single and still living at home. He thought this made me eligible. He thought wrong. I don't mix business with pleasure.

So he fired me with two weeks notice. "Think it over," he said. "Valentine's Day is your last day."

I did think it over. I decided to get even.

Now, you may not know this, but the florist business is a very personal kind of business. You have a lot of regulars.

Our regular customers place standing orders for delivery to observe special occasions like birthdays, anniversaries, Christmas, Mother's Day, and Valentine's Day. Mother's Day is the biggest day in the flower business. Valentine's Day is second. These regular customers are the bread-and-butter customers, the ones that keep us going steadily. Walk-ins are a bonus. After a few years, you get close to customers. You hear about the weddings, the children, grandchildren, funerals, and girlfriends. You become friendly with the customers. That is what gave me the idea.

Every time the boss was out, I worked on our bread-and-butter list. I had everything I needed: addresses, credit card info, and what kind of flowers each preferred. About half of this list was for Valentine's Day. It was a nice big number.

My plan began with Valentine's Day as my target date.

First, I sent the boss's wife Helen a bunch of orchids with a card that read, "Dear Heidi: I can't wait to be with you forever. Love, Ernie."

Then I sent a dozen roses to Heidi, the girlfriend, with a card that read, "Dear Helen: I promise you I will never be unfaithful again. Love, Ernie."

And so on. The two weeks went fast. Ernie still couldn't believe that I had turned him down. He had my replacement standing by.

Valentine's Day arrived. The calls started coming in around noon as I was packing my personal stuff in a box.

Ernie was taking telephone orders for last minute Valentine's Day requests when his wife called.

Whatever she told him, he sat down sweating and breathing hard.

Then Heidi called. She hung up on him.

Things got worse. Husbands began to call. Some threatened to sue. One threatened suicide. Some just threatened to kill Ernie.

Ernie got the picture. He was cornered.

I picked up my belongings and started for the door.

"So long, Ernie," I called out to him, "and Happy Valentine's Day."

With Malice Toward Some

A Dry Run

Brooklyn and Connecticut collided when her Jaguar hit his used BMW. She immediately admitted her responsibility and offered to pay for any damages and inconvenience caused by the accident. Frank instantly liked her openness, a trait he thought lacking in most women. She found him less boring than most men she dated.

Patricia invited him for a cup of coffee to exchange insurance info. The cup of coffee extended into dinner. The fact that they did not know each other somehow made conversation easy. Each made the other comfortable to just be themselves. There was no coyness, no flirting, and no game playing. Something else was happening—and it was pleasant!

They began to see each other for a glass of wine, a new restaurant opening, and gallery openings. They both understood that the relationship was going someplace.

After a few more meetings, he asked her if she would like to set the date.

"Don't rush me. Let's get to know each other better. I am a perfectionist. You have to be patient with that kind of quirk."

"How much better?"

"I'll show you what I like, and you show me what you like. Or I will tell you what I don't like, and you will tell me what you don't like. Let's be open. Let's not have any misunderstandings."

The engagement took their friends by surprise. They all agreed it would never last. Patricia was too much Connecticut, and Frank was too much Brooklyn. He gave her an antique engagement ring harvested from one of the many estate sales he attended. She gave him a Porsche.

"I have never spoiled a man before. Please, humor me."

"Okay," he agreed, "this once. But how shall I spoil you?"

"You will find out if you have the patience," she replied flirtatiously.

He told her he was ready to leave Brooklyn. "I am ready to leave Connecticut," she answered. They agreed to rent an apartment on Manhattan's West Side. The lease was signed, a wedding date set, furniture ordered, and a secret honeymoon hideaway planned.

"It's a good thing the boys from the neighborhood can't see me now," Frank thought. Here he was humoring her one more time.

"I warned you that I am a perfectionist. You still have time to back out." She raised her head to look at him and smiled in anticipation as he positioned himself.

He looked down at her and thought, "How lucky can I get?"

"Come on, Frank, you promised. This will be the last thing I'll ask before the wedding. Honest."

Frank sighed good-naturedly.

Patricia laughed. "There, a little higher. Mmmmm," she purred. "A little to the right. Slowly, slowly. A little lower. That's a nice spot. A little lower, right there," she giggled. "Perfect."

Smiling with satisfaction and relief, Frank screwed the drapery rod into place.

The Mother's Day Gift Dilemma

I was running out of original ideas for Mother's Day gifts.

My mother's only sin, a serious one if you ask me, is her pride when she boasts to her friends about the gifts her children give her. Especially my gifts.

Among the bridge set, she reigns supreme with her stories of my original gifts. I am not quite sure if this has endeared her to the group. I only know that she hints to me in such a way as to suggest that I must keep on being creative and original with my gifts. It is her way, I suppose, of staying one up on her friends.

Sending flowers was a definite no. So was candy. So were scarves. I really have to stretch to stay on top of this problem. Birthdays and anniversaries did not matter. Mother's Day is the most important day for creative giving. It let her shine a little bit more than the other mothers who received flowers and candy and scarves.

Frankly, I was challenged. I didn't want to be done in by giving her an ordinary gift. I had experienced her disappointment with the fruit of the month, book of the month, and dinner of the month certificates. She accepted these gifts quietly without enthusiasm.

My father is good-natured and is happy with just a handshake on Father's Day, which makes it easier for me.

This year marked an unusual breakthrough. The Bloomingdale's catalog featured a Barbara K 30-piece tool kit. A tool kit created for women. The tools have been designed for women's hands. The kit itself looked like an accessory. A woman would not be ashamed to leave the pearl and aqua case on her counter. The kit included various "how to" booklets.

My mother was thrilled with the originality.

First, she repaired the dripping faucet my father never got around to fixing. Next she tackled the running toilet in their basement. Soon she was mixing cement and making a custom glazed ceramic path around the house. She expanded her horizons and began doing electrical work. She rewired the bathroom. There was no stopping her. She offered her services, for free, to her friends, who were amazed at this newfound talent. This kept her busy. This also kept her one up on her bridge pals.

My father, however, surprised me. He was not a good sport through all this. He did not enjoy the jokes that went with this role reversal. His manhood was offended.

I worried. They were drifting apart. They were doing fewer things together.

I thought hard about what to do. His birthday was soon. I had an inspiration.

As a gift for his birthday, I enrolled him in the Culinary Institute of America. He bloomed. He went from omelets to braised venison in a few months. He became a better cook than my mother.

He started cooking for his friends and having tasting parties. He spent a great deal of time tracking down the best, freshest, and most exotic ingredients to add to his menus.

Now my mother is not happy with the jokes about the role reversal. Her womanhood is offended.

I need to rescue the situation.

Their wedding anniversary is in a few weeks. I am giving them a gift certificate to a week-long workshop called "How To Put Zest into Your Marriage!"

It's being held at a nudist camp.

About the Author

Georgia Post was born in Washington, D.C., at a time when closets were for clothes—not for coming out of. Her parents were immigrants from Greece. Georgia's mother cried for three days after Georgia was born because she was a female.

She was valedictorian when she graduated high school.

Her most interesting professional experience was her twelve years as Executive Director of the Cyprus Children's Fund, a sponsorship program for children displaced as a result of the Turkish invasion of Cyprus. Her most challenging experience was to found a nonprofit agency for Greek and Greek American women to deal with domestic violence. Her most gratifying experience was to rediscover her storytelling passion.

She claims she is a 76-year-old woman with a 40-year-old woman struggling to come out.

Her first book *With Malice Toward Some* may or may not be based on people who may or may not have dropped in and out of her life. Only one story is true, but she will not reveal which one.

To order additional copies of

With Malice Toward Some

visit on-line at:

www.savpress.com

and use PayPal
for immediate shipment

or call
1-800-732-3867
Visa/MasterCard Accepted

E-mail us at:
mail@savpress.com
if you have any questions.

All Savage Press books are available at all chain and independent bookstores nationwide. Just ask them to special order if the title is not in stock.